"An emotionally astute [...]
Loves and Other Storie [...]
essential nature of spir [...]
and empathetically expl [...]
Indian women regarding marriage and family life, conveyed
with great care and nuance. What makes the collection so
powerful is this quandary is by no means isolated to any
one culture, making these stories at once culturally specific
and universal, which is an impressive feat of storytelling.
Gullapalli commendably balances a vital perspective on
women's freedom with compelling and relatable tales –
wherever you may live."

Self-Publishing Review, ★ ★ ★ ★

"Launching with a 4/4 review, a collection of short stories
about the search for happiness and the finding of it!
…different approach to address matters arising in modern
society… teaches the need for mental wellness, right
approach to issues, tolerance, marriage, family, values,
and survival. Using humans as practical examples, the
author shows the picture of our lives through the fictional
characters in the book… written in simple diction… applies
to people of all genders and ages… rate the book 4 out of 4
stars because it was an apt, concise, and fascinating read!"

—By onlinebooklovers.org

Three Loves and Other Stories

Lata Gullapalli

BALBOA.PRESS

A DIVISION OF HAY HOUSE

Balboa Press books may be ordered through booksellers or by contacting:

Balboa Press
A Division of Hay House
1663 Liberty Drive
Bloomington, IN 47403
www.balboapress.co.uk
UK TFN: 0800 0148647 (Toll Free inside the UK)
UK Local: (02) 0369 56325 (+44 20 3695 6325 from outside the UK)

Print information available on the last page.

ISBN: 978-1-9822-8457-2 (sc)
ISBN: 978-1-9822-8458-9 (e)

Balboa Press rev. date: 02/26/2022

Dear Angela
with lots of love
& hugs?
& mama
Ruth
:.

"To my three musketeers"

London
June 2023

Three Loves

Yahi hai aazmana to satana kisko kehte hain, adu ke
ho liye jab tum to mera imtehan kyon ho!!

If this is testing waters kind of getting to know, what
is torment? If you have switched allegiance to my rival,
why must I continue to be tested?.

For the first and possibly only time in her life, she was
late. Sia, the perfectly and always-on-time girl, was late.
To be born, that is.

Every day, her mother would wait for the contractions
to begin, closely watched by her grandmother, great aunts
and aunts. All of whom were well versed in the "when is
a woman in labor" signs. And every day they waited in
vain. She was not showing herself, not yet anyway.

Finally, a week late. she emerged, shock of black
hair, huge black eyes, like the giant beautiful fish shapes
that one drew for eyes, and skin smooth, in the colour of
the creamy magnolia in fresh bloom. And kicking and
screaming of course.

Everyone heaved a sigh of relief.

Granny went home to refresh herself with a bath, thank the gods and a good night's sleep now that she had seen the new arrival's face and her daughter was peaceful too. Whatever was the baby thinking, she mused, coming late? In our family?

She is Sia, they all decided. And she was, in every way she was the picture perfect mythological heroine, Sita, in all her beauty, and she radiated an inner spark, an enthusiasm, and energy, much so that heads turned when she walked past and the excitement rose automatically in any group she joined, anywhere she went, kids play groups, school, college, parties....

No one seemed to be envious or feel anything remotely in the nature of the unpleasant green eyed envy either.

It was most unusual- almost a charmed existence.

She grew up with her brother and sister feeling, not unusually, given the attention she drew, that she was a very important part of the world. And her being in it, contributed to it going round.

As she reached her teen years, some things began to register. That it wasn't her that her Father looked for when he came home from work. That she was simply smiled at and then ignored when it came to taking any important decision. Including those that related to her own life. What she should study, what she should wear, what she should eat, whom she should be friends with.

You can't wear jeans- not to college for sure-you can't think of a course in languages, are you going to be a secretary- you can't eat bananas, how many will you eat anyway- why do you hang out with that girl, don't you know she's not great at her studies? And boys, you seem particularly obsessed with!

Soon it became all too routine. It took a big lot of them and sprayed liberally on her often enough, for Sia to notice these barbs. She was so used to letting things like this pass or making an excuse for the other person- every time, her nature was to forget it had happened even, before it happened again. Funny how she began to see them once she stopped to think of what was being said a few times. Guess it's what your mind looks for when it looks for validation or endorsement from family, and when you gloss over, you really do gloss over! And how!

Was she a fool to have thought she had the security, the comfort and the warmth of her parental home? Was it all in only her imagination? Was none of the affection real?

What was it about her, or who she was, or had grown into, that meant a total lack of equality or the sense of justice in what her own dished out to her so frequently. And so freely too. Was there ever a sense of equality between them siblings at all? She was sure she deserved that at the very minimum, but it wasn't there. Aren't we born equal? And the progressive and educated family she thought she belonged to, was surely not discriminating between the sexes.

The strong sense of justice inherent in her, that made her always pause to try and think of the situation from the other person's point of view, told her time and again that she was on the short end of the stick, but she always pushed the thought away and with force. She wasn't prepared to accept this was being done to her by her own. She just wasn't ready for that. Was it because the thought that she was being treated differently, badly and pushed around so much so, it was interfering into her innermost thoughts and making her aware of things she wouldn't give a thought to otherwise.

It wasn't always a case presented for her to prove, by listening to their "well meaning advice", how much she loved her family and so she was ready to do whatever they said and listen to the most outlandish, absurd reasons as to why she couldn't do what she really wanted to do, and especially when she could do it really well. It couldn't be right. What was indeed the point of it all anyway? What could they gain from suppressing her or pushing her around like this? She couldn't even bring herself to think this was indeed true, but she was honest and finally, there it was. The truth laid bare. But with no clues as to why.

She had no answers to her questions and no one to ask them to either.

When it all became too intense for her to handle, Sia began to seek answers and dived in to read philosophy, all the greats she could think of and lay her hands on. Starting with the Bhagavat Gita, which was said to contain the gospel truth in its purest form and worth imbibing and following the way it showed; it was clearly, a way of life for many.

After all she was only eighteen. The stress was beginning to show.To wear her out. The constant need to put on a happy face. To perform whenever she was asked to-make us laugh was a regular task she was given. While she became the joker, she became withdrawn and more silent. Everyone expected her to be the life and soul of any event-much like a jester who comes in and entertains the crowd, almost at will. The will of the others. They would call her to tell them an amusing take or have a laugh or several but as she could see now, clearly, always left her out of any serious feeling of involvement. Make us all laugh, Sia, they would throw at her. Constantly. She began to feel like the standing joke, not the sense of humour variety either.

And come conversation time, it was always like, go and play while we speak of some serious stuff here. Your brain can't handle this and you will only be in the way.

You can't know what's good for you and decide so here's what you need to do. Thats it!!

Sia even went to the extent of trying to make bridges with her family on this clear communication gap- talking to them, after all, was going to take care of it, no? Maybe they didn't see it that way, or really understand what she felt and understood from all these slights. They were her own family, her mother, father, brother and sister- she tried every argument- that she too was old enough, and she too could help in any way. But no- they didn't think so. She still felt shivers down her arms or spine when she remembered how coldly they looked at her and just tossed their heads as if, what would this idiot child come up with next. Wasting our precious time like this. We are totally in the right and don't we know it. They all were so proudly arrogant in their insulting ways.

Making remarks that cut through to her core, were ways she found out later, commonly used to suppress people and done over a period would doubtless destroy every last vestige of pride and self respect she had. That's what bullies did.

And so it went on and on, day after day and year after year.

Her life seemed to resemble the African proverb, *A child who is not embraced by the village will burn it down to feel its warmth.*

Indeed, she began to do more and more to try and win attention, affection, approval, acknowledgement even. Like she was on this massive treadmill and running faster and faster and yet remaining at the same spot. No shred of affection came her way. She was the hamster running on the wheel and thinking she was making progress, whereas all the time she was just going round and round, pretty much in the same place.

No amount of asking, discussing or talking brought her any further or closer to changing how anyone spoke or interacted with her or anything else, for that matter. Not one tiny bit. It was like she was outside the magic circle, looking in through a glass, at all the happy people inside the bubble. There was no way in and no one was inviting her in either.

A great dejection settled on her shoulders, almost a terrible dark despondent truth, one which she could not accept or indeed, escape.

It was the sheer wretchedness of it all. Sia wanted, oh so desperately, for her family to include her, to fold her in, to embrace her in her entirely. Not the crumbs of affection that sometimes came her way, like crumbs that fell off a table at dinner. She was looking for the whole slice of freshly baked and cut bread, toasted and still warm, crisp on the outside, soft on the inside and spread liberally with the fresh butter that gave it a golden tinge and seemed to beckon anyone who saw it to step forward and take that irresistible bite. Chewed with satisfaction wide on their features. That's what she wanted. She deserved it, dammit! In what way was she inferior to be kept at this arms length, she could never fathom a credible response to this.

The wretchedness came from wanting the affection of her family, and trying to keep the hope alive that they will change their minds, perhaps even the next day, maybe.

And all the while knowing, with every fibre of her being, that this will never ever come to pass. They would never change and never see her as she wanted to be seen.

Never wrap her in the warmth of the blanket of their love and affection and hold her so close, she felt safe, secure, cocooned, cared for and part of the family. Her family.

The growing up years are meant to be a whole gazillion of beautiful moments of family time spent in so many wonderful ways, ways that taught the younger ones and prepared them for the life ahead of them and passed the baton from older to younger smoothly, generation to generation. It was a time the members of the family discussed what happened in their lives and told stories of their days so others could laugh, care, console, counsel and just rejoice in the warmth of family. A loving family full of a deep and obvious love for each other.

The love that should be mind blowing in how intense it felt. A love that should be sweeping her up into a giant embrace like a giant whirlwind. A love that should be so powerful one can think one can almost reach a hand out and touch it. A love so overwhelming, it would gather her into the secure family circle and keep her there. A love that flowed like a never-ending giant waterfall that brought fresh water to green the lands in never ending cascades. A love that cared and nurtured her every breath as if the world depended on it. What confidence such a love would give!

But Sia was blessed with the third eye of intuitive understanding and that told her, none of this would ever happen, even if she were to wait for a figurative thousand years.

The wretchedness was indeed a complete one. To know a wonderful family, to have them want not much or very little part of you, anytime. To have a heart full of love for them but they wanted none of it, was enough to send her to the full dregs of despair.

Instead of the closeness she felt a salmagundi of a messy neither this nor that, which defied definition too.

The only way to break out of this was to leave the family home she finally decided. It would be heartbreaking for her. To say goodbye to her family and leave, not because she was going to move away from them and live a life of her own, but to say the goodbye as if it were the final one. Somehow she knew no one was going to follow her with any curiosity or sense of responsibility as to see how she was doing or if she needed any help with anything.

To say a goodbye when someone dies, is indeed gut wrenchingly hard to do, but to do that when the people were alive, thriving and well, but just not interested in engaging in a relationship with her? That took a different level of grit and inner strength. Not that she had some lofty terms or ideals for a relationship. Mutual respect and loads of displays of love and affection in a non judgemental frame was all she was looking for really. Not much to ask for, was it?

She began to unwind from the relationship. Like unravelling a piece of woven thread with many colours intertwined, she began to undo, to cut the thread of each relationship in her mind, with the prayer, that she was liberating, with all her heart and soul, her relative from the bonds that seemed to tie them together until now.

Each strand was cut and the knots inside her seemed

to loosen a little more. She began to feel the urge to go away from the home that had been hers, or so she had thought, for these years.

But how to move and where to go? All attempts to find a job at another place were promptly shot down by her family and living here seemed to be this endless and without limit, repeat of the same feeling of rejection that got her crying inside every time. Like a forever loop!

Sia made her plans. She applied for a job, went about the interviews and conversation stages without letting herself pause for breath, or letting anyone know. She landed herself a teaching position in Hue, a town 2,000 miles away from home and one fine day, announced her move.

Shock, disbelief and absolute arrogant condescension came along, sure as the day follows the night. More than the fact that she had taken the position, which was a good one, doubtless, it was that she had done it on her own, and without that all important involvement and "advice" of her precious high thinking family. That she thought she could even consider deciding any of her life decisions without their diktats was more than they could stomach. They couldn't speak for the towering rage they were all in and a full scale cold war ensued.

She was, in a second, cut off as an outcast, never one to be going anywhere in her life, not worth their royal patronage. She had to blink- to think of her, like that? Seemed so remote. As if it were happening to someone else. She always thought that even if they did not change their brusque and inconsiderate words and attitude to her, her family was still on her side.They perhaps wanted the best for her too, no? How could she stand there and stomach being punched so low and with unerring accuracy, when she needed all the kindness and consideration, if she was to make this tough move out of home, with any measure of success.

Sia was not one to sit around and support those who blamed their parents for all their faults, in fact she was most vocal in asserting that while it may be that gaps in upbringing do occur for some, they can be bridged or overcome by becoming conscious of them and working on overcoming them.

Having said that though, an estrangement from one's parents or siblings is a large and permanent emotional hole that one tends to falls through. What could be done about that?

Well, that was that. It seemed no one was even the slightest bit interested in any more detail or in helping her, so she set herself up for the big moving day.

First love had had a massive heart failure. The heart weakened by so many years of sustained attack, couldn't hold out any longer. It simply gave out.

Sia went along to Hue, settled in her hotel room, got her workplace directions and went along. She made all the necessary paperwork happen and eased herself into the sunshine of building her new world and making her new world her own. With her own unique brand of personality. Sunny side up, that was her. Her brilliant insightful ways of seeing the little paths emerging from the maze of the life in Hue, allowed her to feel at home and lock away the past on the very back burner. Long term memory bits in super cold storage- that was the right thing to do, she felt.

The days were full and busy with work, getting to

know the place as well as settling into her home and the whole newness of being her own master. Doing what she wanted to do. Eating what she wanted to eat. Wearing what she wanted to wear. Teaching the way she wanted to. Talking to people the way she wanted as well.

A few did ask her for a drink after the work day was done, and she did go along as well, sometimes. She quite liked the idea of a good conversation at a local pub over a drink and then each went to their own homes. Seemed such a sensible idea when she was still getting to know people.

And then she met Matt. He was pretty much what she thought she wanted in a companion. She wasn't thinking of any companion, leave alone a lover yet. He was very intelligent, gentle with her, spoke so well and so much about how important it was to have goals, yes, in the plural and how one should go about achieving them. How life's goals could change and how one must realign with them. He was so big, warm and friendly, she felt cocooned in his company. A little spoilt too. Which was a good feeling. After being the parched desert, some life-giving showers of rain couldn't be more welcome. Perhaps it was her intense bereavement for her lost family that had made her all the more needy. She too wanted the gentle hand on her head, and the companion that said he cared. She felt she could be protected against the world. They would be a team. He seemed to respect her words, her work and did not protest at the attention she naturally got even.

There was something that drew them together. His dislike of spending much money while he happily put large amounts into her purse without her knowing, because she may need some suddenly; or his being a total mess and a fully disorganised one at that; or the fact that he just seemed to wait for people around him to do things he should really be doing for himself; none of these rang any bells in her.

Their initial days together were full of joy, togetherness and discovery, Sia thought he was as enthused as her. Wasn't he?

She sensed the reluctance to take her advice, or tap her knowledge on anything, even a simple household matter, which she prided herself on being aware of, just like she was immensely proud of all she had learned at work. She was highly respected for her abilities and sought after for advice, ever so often. People would call her at all times of the day to take her advice, her direction or simply her view on anything and everything, and with the complete faith that she would give shed the much needed light, on the issue at hand. Even when she said she wasn't very familiar with the subject, they still felt her huge range of deep and complete understanding of most things, would throw up myriad possibilities and that itself would allow a path to be foraged, even in the most downbeat of times. This confidence in her was self reinforcing and had spread simply by word of mouth, not from her ever speaking of what she did or said, and that gave her a certain surety of her ability in that direction. This was further enhanced, if that were possible, when they come back and told her how things worked out and thanks to her timely help and advice.

Matt, on the other hand, never asked her about something, even when he knew she was very familiar with it. He chose to ask other people and many times it was in her presence. She never made a scene, but when she asked why he did that later, he always accused her of being needlessly prickly. Anyway he was just asking and of course that he would ask who he liked. He didn't really think he could trust her knowing so many things really, could he?

She used to be stunned into silence and then the cycle began, of crying it out and trying explaining to him how she knew what she did, followed by requests that he could rely on her. She was most trustworthy and all that. Throughout this, Matt used to nod his head and say yes, yes, of course I rely on you and will take your help, but he never did.

Sia tried to put it down to the newness of the relationship, his anxiety about what he needed to know, he was tired, anything really. She was so much in love. A cynic may have explained it as she was in love with the idea of being in love, and she, for all her talent, was no cynic.

She was so much in love, she couldn't think or do anything when Matt came into the room, or even if he was in the house. Even if she so much as thought of him, and that was often enough, she couldn't concentrate on anything else. She couldn't focus on anything else if he was in the house. She couldn't read a book if he was in the same room. She just wouldn't be able to concentrate. Her entire being was like it was on a high alert and that made her suppress every need of hers with force. She wasn't sensitive to her own needs or thoughts or wants at all. She felt anything she liked or looked at doing, even the simplest things like the way she liked her tea, seemed to melt into things completely unimportant. It was sacrifice of all of her beautiful life as she knew it and she didn't even really know it yet.

Her whole world seemed to revolve around him. And he was very open to directing her as to what she should do and what she shouldn't. She should come home before him and make sure the food was ready. She should make sure his clothes were laundered and ready. She should take no calls from work when he said so. She couldn't make plans to meet friends by herself as it was time together she was picking out of, but he could just go out and stay late, even without informing her, leave alone asking her. And so on the list went.

The complaints spilt over into their moments in bed as well, which for her drove something quite steely and sharp into her very core and kept twisting it this way and that, each time he "analysed" her "behaviour". She was too forward, she initiated sex. She was too rough on him, she kept hurting him. There was no way she could claim tiredness when he was in the mood- that would be a beginning of a sulk and a tantrum which ended with her acquiescing, and feeling used and broken, afterwards. Where was this going, she used to think. I don't always point out what's not going well, why must he? And am I not supposed to have the physical pleasure of being made love to? Of someone finding me attractive? He used to praise the way I looked all the time initially. I don't look any different now, she thought. What makes him say I look ugly or fat or unattractive- just so I shut up and move away one more time and he gets his way.

It felt like the woodcutters axe heaving blows on the strong trunk again and again, with mighty force and the chips were flying, weakening the tree all the time. Soon it would reach the point where the proverbial final blow would bring the entire tree of their relationship down.

It was beginning to show that it was never possible to fully satisfy him anyway. He seemed to have the 'but' ready to be inserted into anything good he said, if he ever did, at any rate. He reserved the right to fly into a towering rage, and erupt no matter where they were. At home, in a public place or at someone else's house. He would not lose a micro second to speak his mind. Each word would be a whiplash and one that meticulously stripped her mentally, of every semblance of decency or respect. He did not believe in mincing any words either. The choicest were available for him to choose and use, all designed to make her feel small and absolutely and overwhelmingly insignificant. It became farcical for her to make excuses for him every time, because being honest, as she was, to see Matt's behaviour for what it was, left her feeling bewildered and at a loss to explain where his aggressive overreactions were coming from. He was supposed to be in love with her too, wasn't he? Didn't anyone who loved another, do everything they could, to show that love and respect and care, especially if they felt their partner was doing something wrong. Didn't that situation call for a most "handle with care" attitude. We do point out the errors and voice our doubts but only with a liberal dose of love and affection and deep underlying respect. What about all those authors on marriages that advocate spouses should speak of five good things for every not so good thing they point out, every single time. Was that just hogwash meant for books and the supposed sops that believed in that sort of thing?

All her insecurities that were all around her during her growing up years, had left a confidence that was already teetering towards a record low level, and this only exacerbated her showing up at the rock bottom again.

She felt positively revolted with this sort of violent dressing down for little or no reason, without any attempt by Matt to have a conversation, or to do a quick fact check, first. Something she had seen so much of at her parental home and found so very demeaning and disrespectful. Why would anyone claiming to be so much in love, try

23

to shut up or put down their partner with such singular lack of respect, was beyond her understanding. Was the purpose to shut the partner up and how they did it did not matter? How could it not matter?

Respect came before love or anything else for her. And should also for everyone else, so she fully believed.

She fought like a caged animal to bring their relationship back from this brink of this abyss that it was now sitting on, ready to fall in. She wanted, with all her heart and soul, to have the relationship with Matt, for him to love and care for her as he did in the first days. All the wonderment and adoration that made their early days of discovering each other, such precious beautiful memories. She fought but every time it was another blow and another nail into the coffin that was going to seal their relationship in it forever and take it to a never land. Perhaps the netherworld. She felt herself weakening and becoming more dejected and more hopeless as the days passed.

The sunny Pollyanna she was, the bright young and beautiful sunbeam she was, was getting buried slowly but surely, under the layers of hurt and a sense of defeat. She put all her might into stopping or stemming the rot, but it just didn't work.

She, who had stepped out of her parental home, with only hope to guide her, had dared to turn her face to the sun. She had dared to hope again. Dared to think she could love and cherish, the forever kinds at that. She had stepped out of the misery and given herself a good shake off, of all the baggage that she had allowed herself to be laden with all those years. She had dared to expose herself to another person and allowed him in her innermost thoughts.

Had she been desperate to find affection, having had received so little of it from her family? No, she went over her thoughts and came to that conclusion. No, she had not rushed into this. She was not looking for any partner or friend even, and with Matt, it grew slowly. And cautiously. She was sure she had been looking for any warning signs and indeed there were none whatsoever, at the time. She was confident of her own cautious approach to things, and sure that some red flags would have appeared if any cracks came up at all.

She had read somewhere that the beginning of a relationship with an abuser is often wonderful. Of course it is; otherwise you would probably get out of the relationship immediately. Forceful, threatening, and degrading behaviour is often disguised and delivered in a humorous way, a seemingly reasonable tone, or in concerned loving words. Most often the one at the receiving end remains largely unaware of the larger dynamic, and feeling completely confused as to why they feel so bad about it. Over time, the abuser gains more power and control in the relationship, while the victim becomes a shell of his or her former self, often developing some form or other, of depression and anxiety, and sometimes even turning to unhealthy outlets to soothe the pain.

It is the less overt and subtle tactics that cause us to question ourselves, our reality, and our worth, keeping us more dependent on our abuser and making it less likely we will leave. It is psychological bullying day in and day out, from a person who knows you intimately.

Too many people remain unaware and vulnerable to mistreatment in a relationship, and it's critical to start getting answers to these important questions; What are the not so obvious early warning signs of an unhealthy relationship? What is acceptable treatment, and what isn't? Where do you draw that line? How do you recover and develop your confidence in your relationships? What does a healthy relationship even look like? If you're looking for greater respect, satisfaction, and happiness in your relationships, both now or going forward, it's imperative to educate yourself so that you can set your relationship standards bar higher.

Having loved him with all her heart and pledging to do so till eternity and back, she was not going to say anything hurtful to him. Not now, not ever. The hurt was hers alone and she was going to take it with her.

Her note to Matt was succint.

Dear Matt

For the first time in my life, with lot of hesitation, I have decided to think of my own feelings as paramount to my life and as the guide to what I will do in the future-

The fact that I have taken so many years both before and after marriage to arrive at this decision should be enough to show how long a rope I have been giving you, and my state of health and mind should show how that rope was, and is being put to use.

You always dithered on a maybe for everything and took absolutely no decision. That way you thought you reserved the right to criticise, and severely, everything I did, or was starting to do, while you wouldn't even decide, leave alone do anything. It is amazing I continued to take the initiative for every single thing, in spite of knowing the barrage of criticism, mean, hurtful and really lowdown in its choice of words, was coming my way, in complete generosity, and with relentless precision, from you.

I was always the professional, bringing in my professional approach to my housewife's role as well, seeking to maintain my respect for you, even when you were being an absolute cad, but you never thought once before saying anything, however untrue or unspeakable it was. You said it all anyway, simply to shut me up. And you knew my pride would make me shut up. There would be a sorry from you sometime later, and then off we went to the next incident.

Bette Davis said in her autobiography, The lonely life, "It has been by experience that one cannot, in any shape or form, depend on human relations for lasting reward. It is only work that truly satisfies".

But to me it was always a multitude of relationships that were around me, a weave of a colourful and intense fabric, strong, yet caring and gentle, that it was the warmest of cloaks to soothe me at troubled times and the coolest of balms when I was needy. The absoluteness of my commitment to the team "us" was never in question, was it ever? To me some things were beyond and above the trust and complete and implicit faith barrier. Never to question and never to doubt.

But for you, it was about not letting me have any expectations from you, as you reserved the right to get involved or help or whatever, on a case to case basis, while all the while having the highest expectations from me, on commitment or effort or willingness- you name it.

You put everything up in the air and every single one

of those cardinal principles that should have been the bedrock of our relationship were constantly on parade and in question. For me though, not for you, and time and time again, I found myself proving my commitment or proving my support or love or feelings, which I found most degrading, to say the least. This made me feel like I was being stripped naked and put under a strong spotlight, at will, and I had to fight, to prove myself, and in so doing, to earn every item of my clothing back, to put on.

This, happening totally and regularly, especially at will, was the proverbial water falling constantly on the same spot on a stone. Even the toughest stone wears off over time and then a simple blow breaks it apart and smashes it to smithereens. The dust from a stone that has been blown to smithereens cannot be assembled back into the fine, proud and strong stone it once was. Try as I might, I couldn't subject myself to this level of degradation, for the immense love, respect, or anything else. I just couldn't. It goes against my core and against every fibre of my being.

To you I was the housewife pretending to be the

professional. And not the other way round. How two people can see the same thing, and from the opposite ends, so it is the complete reverse of the others' view.

You may be right in saying that I am a failure at relationships and that I am the one that has a problem with virtually everyone, or the relationships I am in. Since I seem to have failed to make my family happy and I failed to make you happy as well. But one cannot make anyone happy or sad. And it is not a philosophical statement either. It is just the simple truth. People can be happy or sad only based on what they allow themselves to feel. At any time. That is the power the mind has over the emotions.

I am content in the knowledge that I have tried to the best of my ability and capacity, with all enthusiasm, to build, maintain and sustain, every single relationship that I have. After all, at the end of the day, any relationship only looks like what we feed it, what we put into it, isn't it? TLC all the way or none of that- it will show eventually when the one that endures stops enduring. And for what, one may ask? One endures for love, for respect, for concern or for affection- one does not endure to be battered each time- to be mentally abused for no earthy reason.

I have to leave, for my own self and for my care and compassion for myself.

I wish you all of the very best.

Sia.

She moved into her flat that very afternoon.

Sia was filled with the deep sense of loss. It seemed like yet again, the deep and undying love and the heart that had nurtured these, and indeed at one time, immeasurable feelings, seemed to give way and suffer a fatal cardiac arrest. This second love too, that had so filled Sia's heart, it seemed immeasurable, now fell flat and had had the massive and fatal haemorrhage, putting it on its way to an early grave.

Man re Tu kaahe na dheer dhare! Tu nirmohi moh na jaane jinka moh kare!

Utna hi upkaar samajh koi, jitna Saath nibhaade, Janam Mara ka mel hai sapna yeh sapna bisraade, Koi ne sang mare....

Dear heart of mine, you need to be stronger. You, who are unaware of the hidden agendas of those whom you love. You need to just be grateful for the companionship, as much as it is, no more, as even I know, the soul is eternal and will not die, and no one will die with it either.

That Sia felt empty and bereft of all feelings seemed to be an understatement. She wasn't sure she had the courage to try even at the very basic level, to pick herself up and move forward.

She had read somewhere that when the more obvious markers of abuse are not being met, people are often left to question themselves and their sanity.

Like Olivia Fane said, "Falling in love is like reaching out to another human being with a sense of privilege and care. Monogamy is the ideal situation as then you are free from the constant thought of sex, to be able to love. The entire world that you inhabit, your family friends and the earth sky stars and then some! It allows you to love the person you are married to- not because they are lean, rich, tanned or for the earth shattering sex, but because you take their spectacles off when they fall asleep and put the reading book they have, away, and, by that, enter the world they are absorbing, momentarily. That is true intimacy. When you can share the others' world, silently and peacefully. That's what makes you a couple, a whole and complete pair."

The psychological term for the defence mechanism is that which makes a person cancel out or remove an unhealthy destructive or otherwise threatening thought or action by engaging in contrary behaviour. But in reality, even if we know the reality deep down, we do the contrary.

Do we not do want to believe in our partners, that we choose to unknow things? Unsee things?

That sometimes the truth of who and what we married, gets distorted by the description of what we want to be married to.

It is like the eclipse that comes along and thinks it can block it and does obliterate the mighty Sun, but being the shining light the Sun is, the brilliance of the it seeps through around the edges and sure enough, there is light, plenty of it all around.

A woman who is strong and capable may be pushed down, knocked over, passed over and belittled for the very ability she has, and has acquired with good, honest effort, combined with enormous capability. She may be blocked for a while even, but the light finds the gap and comes shining through. There are innumerable women who are cut off in each and every venture they have started, set up, established and achieved magnificent successes. Or relationships like marriage too.

They say devotion in a temple, detachment in a cremation ground and love in times of distress are very easy to find, but they don't last long- the moment we leave the temple, cremation ground or are no longer in distress or difficulty - the feeling disappears. Leaving us to wonder what we whether we imagined the feelings in the first place.

The truth is Compassion is an action word with no boundaries. Fierce self-compassion is the kind action we take in order to prevent ourselves from being harmed by ourselves or others. It's a powerful resource to make changes in our lives from a place of love.

We see in society that unconscious biases are so high and so implicit in every aspect of the man-woman relationship. For the man, though, the fact that the woman also has or may have a bias against him matters little or not at all because the man has all the institutions backing him. Every law that has been framed has been in his favour. Perhaps there have been some changes recently, but historically it's been a "man's world" in every way.

The woman never had any such backing. Nor earlier. Not now.

And that's the key difference.

Sia caught her reflection in the mirror and looked at herself. What she saw there was the woman she knew. The woman that had been pushed down repeatedly. The scars were raw and she saw her lip wobble. The beginning of a need to cry. Out loud and at everything around her. To cry out the suffering that was in her soul. To scream with each whiplash of words she had listened to and still held together, for so long. To let the impotent hurt and rage flow out of her like the volcano that had built up to boiling point over the past years. The physical self she had taken to ignoring as it wasn't attractive enough to Matt anymore. The mind that housed her thoughts and gave her direction for the actions that she was insulted and belittled for time and again. Old hurt and new seemed to mingle and made her want to wrench them from inside her and throw them far away, so they may never bother her again.

And then she stopped. She saw the Sia that she was. Always had been. She looked in the mirror and saw herself and a little smile played at the corner of her mouth. She thought of herself, her achievements, single handed and with no help or support, her numerous awards and accolades she had gained over the years and the loyal group of friends she had made too. All of these seemed to be rooting for her. To be saying, "Go find your rainbow, Sia. We are with you." Her smile widened. She was like in a trance now. Positivity seemed to radiate from her reflection to her. She smiled at the lovely person in the mirror in front of her. Here was a love that was hers to have, and hers to keep. Her inner self, so beautiful and so serene, so replete with divine energy, the kind that flows in and out of ourselves and in and out of all this surrounding us.

As Damian Lewis said about Helen McCrory

It's the fire in my eyes, And the flash of my teeth, The swing in my waist

And the joy in my feet, I'm a woman, Phenomenally, Phenomenal woman,

That's me!

This oneness with the universe was a lovely melody. Tuneful and soul stirring.

Sia thought for a moment. When she meditated, she tried to reach the inner self, and when she did that, she is suddenly filled with the brilliance of inner light, like a third eye opening, a sense of lightness, of incredible peace and calm that makes her feel like she was melting into the surrounding energy. She became one with the universal energy. She became one with the cosmic force that flows seamlessly from her to everything around her and back through her. It energised and filled her with a divine power that makes her one with the supreme. And then she lost the need to perform other rituals or seek out the Lord in prayer or in holy spots. The energy that flows through her is vital as it is intuitive and while binding her to the world, yet liberates her from it.

It is an energy that is to be experienced to understand. It takes time to be able to harness the vast extent of the flows, and the highly intuitive thoughts that come to mind as a result. The solutions to problems or even the calls for help that come from around her.

This is what perhaps, the yogis or the seers say when they tell us they can sense what is happening in our lives and are able to give us direction for what is to happen as well. They have simply achieved oneness with the energy around them in the universe and that's when they are able to intuitively figure out what the disciple or any person for that matter, needs.

Sia thought, "I have achieved the level of detached attachment, that I am one with the universal energy while continuing with the life in this world. This is the beginning of a love affair of a lifetime."

She had found her third love.

Magic

Raat yun dil me teri khoyi hui yaad aaye

Jaise veerane me Chupke se bahaaar aaa jaaye

Jaise sehera me haule se chale baad e naseem

Jaise beemar ko be vajaha karaar aaa jaaye

Your long lost memories come to warm my heart at night

Just like the spring that brings blooms quietly in the desert

Like slowly, the breeze moves in the desert

Like a sick person, for some unknown reason, finds peace.

Shruti walked in the door as usual, dropped her keys into the bowl and slipped her shoes off. God, she was tired. But there was something today that was different. She ran a hand over the back of her neck and stretched herself as she walked.

It had been a usual day- long and hard negotiation for the term sheet. It was always a tough one to agree on the value to place on a company! The buyer wanted less and the seller more- classic case of bargaining, holding the hands of both and taking them through this term sheet partnership. This was what she loved to do and did well, mergers and acquisitions. It wasn't just a job for her, it was first love.

Yes, she thought, for the zillionth time, love.

There it was again- the feeling that had been following her all day.

She saw it in her eyes when she caught a sight of herself in the mirror during the intense negotiation- she had an extra sparkle, an intensity with which she spoke- both Clive and Hemendra were a bit on the back foot today. Whenever she spoke they listened and agreed- without much argument either. She was speaking a lot more forcefully than usual- goodness knew she was aggressive enough at work...

They must have wondered what was eating her?

She was wondering what it was as she poured herself her usual glass of Chianti. She picked up the glass and looked at it strangely- as if she expected to see something else- there it was again! The odd feeling she couldn't quite put her finger on!

She looked at the bottle- Castillo de Verrazano- same as always. So what was it?

Shruti sat down in her favourite chair and prepared to go over her day in her mind- it was a habit she had taught herself- go over anything she did or said or others did or said, even something that just seemed to have happened, and she could break it up to arrive at the beginning- what set it off, what started it. She liked to fully analyse and understand why what happened when it did. It gave her great comfort.

She felt she simply had to find out what it was that started off this unsettled feeling. It was not an unpleasant unsettledness- more like an old familiar ache, an old and so very well known warmth in her, a so very well loved touch.......

And then it struck her- it was the ice cream van she saw this morning on her way to work!

With this realisation, the magic that was lurking on the edges of her day washed over her, swept over her, was all around her now- it came over to take her in its arms and envelop her totally, like a warm cocoon, a safe haven, like the embrace of her lover holding her so so so very close, as if he would never let her go!

She did not fight it any more. She sat back and let the magic take over her.

And it did. It swept over her, took her riding high, all the waves of the knowing, the caring, the wanting, the loving, and the utter and complete surrender she had felt in those magical days and nights!

Today it seemed to be a day to go back, back to the very beginning of her magic story. The story of Shekar and Shruti.

Both were born and brought up in Madras, as Tam-Brahms, as Tamil Brahmins are known. Their upbringing in the so called progressive upper middle class families, who were open to boy meets girl in a different setting and even "daring to meet" before marriage.

The way they had been brought up, though, neither of them would have thought of setting up their own match for marriage. It was just not done that way.

For them, their parents were friends of friends and when they met at one of the official functions all bureaucrats seem to go to, they sat over glasses of whisky and said to each other,

Pandidlam- which was simply, let's do it!! Let's get the children married off!!

And so, simply put, they were engaged to be married.

All the paraphernalia of a South Indian wedding needed to be arranged and all boxes checked- because though they, as parents, were totally progressive and against pomp and show, it was needed to show their relatives and friends how well they could celebrate their children's wedding.

Shruti and Shekar had a few weeks before the wedding date so they went through the list of all types of "allowed" reasons to meet, like shopping, or someone was visiting and they would like to see the girl and so on.

Meet they did, but both were tongue tied virgins in a completely virgin landscape too. Funnily enough, even then, each expected the other to understand what they wanted without really saying it.

There was no question of romantic hand holding.

Their dates were out of the world. On the first "shopping trip" they were walking through the museum grounds on pantheon road and were stopped by policemen. The overzealous madras policemen separated them and kept asking Shruti, Yenna Madam, Is this boy known to you? Is he not troubling you? You look like a girl from a "good" home?

With great difficulty they convinced the policemen that they were indeed already married and went home. Didn't dare mention it to the parents.

Another time, they had coffee at the Dakshin restaurant in the Adayar Park as the Sheraton was called, and Shekar thought he should take the matter into his own hands, being the man, he should be more "knowledgeable". He was being a little more adventurous than usual, and decided to tell Shruti how much he liked her.

So he started off saying he wanted to tell her a story about a girl and a boy and somehow turned it into their story. As it happened he got carried away and excited too by the end of the story so when he finished the story and they were getting up to leave, he suddenly said, "I can't leave"."

"And why not," she said, "it's getting late now.".

"I just can't- I have gone all hard down here" he said and showed a shocked Shruti her first glimpse of something gone hard, albeit trouser clad-

Moments of panic followed, with both thinking out what they could do- should they sit it out or should they leave anyway- but how could he walk with a 90 degree angled gun in his pants?

Shruti was so angry- why would he tell a story like that about someone else and then turn it into their own story and what on earth, was this going hard business?? She told him to just adjust it and start walking as they couldn't wait indefinitely for normalcy to return!

Shekar looked at her and said, "I can't deflate it, you know!"

And it was so very funny, in a minute they were laughing like schoolchildren...

They decided he should hold her office files against himself and walk out- they forgot about the protocol ridden madras restaurant waiters and cashiers- bills were presented to only the men and the men and only the men had to settle them.

So here was Shekar balancing the files against himself with one hand trying to pay the bill with the other- it was so very funny trying to pay the bill with one hand and the cashier wondering why he did not put the files down while he got the money out.

Shruti was laughing so much by the time they got out of the restaurant, the cashier was convinced there was something wrong with her!

They talked about everything but themselves and each other after that-

Their virgin innocence and ignorance took a quick dip into wisdom when they saw an article in the Femina magazine that said, "research" has shown that couples need not have sex every day to be in and to remain "in love forever"!

They both oohed and aahed over this bit of gyan-knowledge- coming their way!

They got married in true South Indian style with 23 dishes on the menu at lunch and so also for dinner. None of the dishes repeated, of course.

Going to live with the In laws was precisely that, in laws and that meant lots of rules- not the simplest of living, even for ones with progressive in laws, as they soon found out.

All meals had to be taken together, and protocol was strict, speak only when spoken to and sit and talk with everyone when they, the others, were awake. No question of going out for dinner or even a coffee- and of course forget about having a lie in on Sunday morning.

Meals were at 11 am sharp....

Shekar and Shruti were just wanting to be with each other- they were getting used to being together and getting to know each other's ways of doing things -realising that not capping the toothpaste tube is reality and bringing up males in South Indian households means they not only do nothing, they know how to do nothing, perfectly. And of course, the bride, the daughter in law, who has been the princess at her own home, with her mum shooing her out of the kitchen or keeping her away from chores saying you will do this later anyway-is actually meant to know how to do everything and perfectly too. Shruti did not think 'anyway' meant after marriage.

Overnight, she was supposed to know, how to make a bed, keep house, make tea for visitors and help cook meals, chapatis needed to be round- and- no kidding-mom in law doesn't even serve the dosa to her little prince, (who is 25+) if the edge is slightly broken.

Virginity meant there was very high excitement but very little idea what to do about it- they knew as much as 10 standard kids about biology because that's where they both had stopped biology as a subject at school.

Trying to discover each other in a few hours in the bedroom and without speaking or making a sound was the cleverest way to impart a lesson on abstinence perhaps.

So they tried their best to keep their heads cool and went to work at night silently- as quietly as they could-but they got interrupted, called out urgently, anything at all, all too often and, frustration, in big bold letters was beginning to nod gently in their direction.

Love making, if it could be called that, was either silently achieved or with all the trying to keep it quiet fumbling, more often than not, given up. Some sound outside either on the road or in the house would make them totally stiffly aware and there of course, was the passion- in the tube!!

Then came a twist in their newly wedded lives. An offer to work in Bombay, as it was called in the old days for him and loads of potential jobs for her.

They moved.

They spent three months in a hotel, looking for an apartment. As children of bureaucrats, they were used to massive accommodation with running water and electricity, bang in he middle of any town, any city.

But here they were in Bombay trying to find a place to live and there seem to be none available with two bedrooms and two bathrooms..... Didn't know why, but they needed that many rooms as a minimum.

A flat in Bandra happened and things seemed to fall into place. The corporate trappings with cars for both arrived too and they were off. Shekar and Shruti had arrived in the city of dreams and begun their climb onto their corporate ladders.

Amazingly quick learners, they soon mastered the way of working in Bombay and were getting totally comfortable. Bonuses started rolling in.

Weekends were off work and time to go around the city or hang out with friends.

Life was beginning to feel like sex on toast....

One Saturday they had lunch and decided to do desert-butter scotch ice cream for a change.

Both sat with their bowls, licking their spoons.

Shruti looked at Shekar and in an instant the minx had spooned ice-cream and flicked it on to Shekar. Before he could realise and react, she had put her cup down and leant over him, to lick it off him.

It was like a wall breaking. A dam bursting. In every way.

Suddenly both of them were spooning icecream on to the other and licking it off- they were on a high- as if they had found the magic key to their own special private world.

All these months of circling around the issue of how to make their nights and days more passionate and intensely satisfying seemed to have found the magic answer in the simple ice cream. Butter scotch it was, all the way !!

It was as if someone had opened the door to their world of passion and pushed them headlong in through it.

They couldn't seem to get enough of it- the ice cream nor of each other.They kept tumbling to the bed together, over and over and reaching the heights of absolute raw passion, with intensity, with abandon, with grace, with fluidity, with a surety in their need and in their new ability to take each other on the ride.

All the way to the top and climax together. They fitted each other's bodies like they were moulded into them. The need to drive deep into her was so strong, Shekar almost hesitated, but Shruti was not afraid anymore.

Together they came and came again. There was a new found intimacy, and a brand new set of rules to play by. The main one being try everything. Now that they have mastered the first position right.

Him on top, her on top, impossible seeming kamasutra stuff 69, 89- they went through all of it. Wonderfully together and without any explanations as to why one wanted to try one way or another.

This was truly the lap of marital bliss. They were not concerned with anyone or anything else any more.

Theirs was a magical world full of tremendous and superbly intense passion. They tried the showers, the couch, the kitchen counter, the lift.

They were even sometimes late for work. Some weekends they barely stepped out of bed. Shekar and Shruti glowed in each other's love making skills. It was as if they needed to try and outdo the last time by an intense supernova for an orgasm.

All the books, they suddenly remembered reading, were true. Passion and love making was such a pleasurable act of togetherness, they never thought of loving and living any other way.

Once, when, driving home in the Bombay monsoon's three hour traffic jams, Shekar was trying to keep calm while he was watching Shruti fret over the long time it was taking- he just reached over and kissed her. They were so busy kissing away, they did not notice the car in front had gone into the pot hole and not moved out in time. And Shruti's foot was no where near the brake!

Bang!! They hit the car in front-

A crowd gathered and the indignant owner of the other car too came marching out to give a "piece of his mind" to this lady driver-

Gone, they thought, we've had it!! The crowd on senapati bapat marg was hard core conservative- that about summed up the description of the setting. Couldn't have picked a worse place to have this incident-

Woman driver and kissing in the car!!

And lo behold- the crowd circled the other driver and took him apart for careless driving-

Such careless driving that too in Bombay rain and look at poor madam in the car behind- look at her- is having to be so disturbed- while she was trying to drive her car home quickly!!

Of course she needs to be allowed to drive away, so go on Madam, you are already delayed by this useless driver!

Shruti and Shekar could not believe their ears and could not hold their laughter back either. Both jumped into the car and drove off as quickly as they could.

From then on they tried their best to kiss when they were driving but would end up laughing so much they could never manage.

Life had never been so good.

What could be better than have a friend for a soulmate and lover and be able to express oneself in every possible way and feel so much enriched by every moment spent together, every hour, every day.

They reached a stage in their loving where they were content sitting holding hands and watching a film, as spending the weekend ravenously feeding their bodily hunger with loads and loads of gentle, stormy, intense, overwhelmingly passionate and intimate lovemaking.

The offer came suddenly. One fine morning Shekar's boss called him and said, in his pucca sahib style, "My boy, you have been doing amazingly well here and the Regional Office in Singapore has asked me to send you there as they need someone like you to shake up their global client accounts."

"It is such a pleasure for me to send you there especially since all these years the RO has been telling us how to run the India business and now you will be going there to be teaching them how to run their own business!!"

Even as they tried to swallow the bit about the job location, and what it would do to their lives, Shekar was all set to say goodbye to the job.

Shocked as she was, Shruti had to make him see the sense in the move for his career, for what he was trying to do. It was the absolute disaster in terms of timing, but when did opportunities come in complete family packages ?

The number of stories going round of people moving and some just moving with no concern for the partner, some drawing lots as to who would be the prime mover this time round or some taking turns as to whose career was more important at this stage, were all too close to not feel for those people.

All these stories, Shekar and Shruti used to listen, recount and laugh over but now they were in it too.

Try as she might, Shruti could not get herself to just quit and move. She was just beginning to move into the position she was working hard for and so richly deserved.

With the economic crisis in Singapore, there was zero chance of her being hired nor any hope of being given a position as senior as she was enjoying here in Bombay.

She was being torn apart inside with the impending separation but there was nothing she could do or wanted to do even.

They both felt like they were caught in the headlights and could only stand still.

Somehow she did make him see the sense of not throwing away his job.

Then the accusations of "you don't love me enough to leave all this and come with me" began- it was all getting way too much for both of them.

Neither could express what they wanted to do themselves leave alone have a plan for the other person to follow. They could not say how much their own careers, built with so much effort meant to them, nor could they put a value on the total oneness they felt now. It seemed odd that two parts of a whole would now be in different countries and not be in the same city, meeting everyday.

The need to see, touch, be with each other was so great, it was not felt as a need anymore, it was clear. They both had made it a - taken for granted- part of their lives.

How does one say goodbye to parts of oneself, neither had any clue where to begin and how to go about it.

The best way, it would seem, was to be quick with the move and that, perhaps, would not prolong the agony for both of them.

They both managed to say goodbye and he left for Singapore and she stayed back in Bombay.

Staying with her work was the best thing she could have done. She was always able to concentrate and give her best, even in all those beautiful love filled days. Clients were ecstatic to have her manage their deals as she never wanted to go home or take calls or time off even.

They did try and call each other a couple of times but what could they say beyond how are you kind of stuff. How do you tell yourself or an integral part of you that you need him or her? Where would you start and how would you say it? And what if that half didn't come to you?

Slowly the urge to call receded too and everything seemed normal to everyone else.

Butterscotch never came to her home again.

Shruti dragged herself to the present and took a deep swallow of her wine.

This trip down the magic memory lane was precious and yet she needed to put it away and stay in the present!!

There was no point in going on in this fashion waltzing in memory lane!!

There was a beep beep on her mobile- an sms? At this hour ?

Shruti was almost certain it was Mr Paranoid, Clive, coming out with some nuance which simply must be incorporated into the term sheet even before the morning!!

She placed her glass on the table and reluctantly picked up the 'phone. The message was from an unknown number.

"Care for some ice cream? Just open the door!!"

And there stood Shekar, leaning on the door frame with a tub of butterscotch in his hand! Happy birthday, he said !

Shruti stood still for a moment and then said, we have fifteen minutes before the others arrive for the party- they looked at each other and smiled- fifteen minutes !!

Magic- that's what it was always between them, Magic!!

Soul Energy

Jab nahīṇ tum tõ tasavvur bhī tumhārā kyā zaroor

Uss-sé bhī kehdõ ké yéh taqleef kyõṇ farmāyé hai?

*Of what avail is your imagination when you yourself
are invisible?*

*Tell her, she need not trouble herself even with this
kindness!]*

- Jigar

A deep feeling of gratitude can emerge, as we open to
the experience of being helped.

Most of us pride ourselves on our self-sufficiency.
We like to be responsible for taking care of ourselves and
pulling our own weight in the world. This is why it can
be so challenging when we find ourselves in a situation in
which we have to rely on someone else. This can happen
as the result of an illness or an injury, or even in the case
of a positive change, such as the arrival of a newborn. At
times like these, it is essential that we let go of our feeling

that we should be able to do it all by ourselves and accept the help of others.

The first step is accepting the situation fully as it is. Too often we make things worse either by trying to do more than we should or by lapsing into feelings of uselessness. In both cases we run the risk of actually prolonging our dependency. In addition, we miss a valuable opportunity to practice acceptance and humility. The ego resists what is, so when we move into acceptance we move into the deeper realm of the soul. In needing others and allowing them to help us, we experience the full realisation that we are not on our own in the world. While this may bring up feelings of vulnerability, a deep feeling of gratitude may also emerge as we open to the experience of being helped. This realisation can enable us to be wiser in our service of others when we are called upon to help.

It takes wisdom and strength to surrender to our own helplessness and to accept that we, just like every other human being, have limitations. The gifts of surrender are numerous. We discover humility, gratitude, and a deepening understanding of the human experience that enables us to be that much more compassionate and surrendered in the world.

This is one such story. When I lived this story, one that takes a life of its own, and quite dramatically and in a most unimaginable way, I was in the middle of the whirl of world - other world and not knowing which way to go, which one to believe, which to rely on. This is a tale between me and her, two of us who were perhaps attached in a realm beyond this visible world, and one that took almost more than I could give….

She came with me- just as she's been - with me for over a year now....she was one with the song - every nuance she took in- she blessed her lovely children- swept around her family and friends!!!

She was so happy to see everyone.

For so long- over a year now- she has been with me-worried about her home- her family. I felt each moment of her restlessness.

It started well before she was a free spirit.

The agony, the fear, the worry of what would happen...

Every time I did my best reassure her it would be alright and that she should not worry like this.

This was different!! This time she was content! She was happy! She was saying thank you to me... the crazy girl.... For enduring her fears. For not thrusting her away from me and shutting her out. For going out there and letting her see for herself how her loved ones had found their feet, making me give them the help they needed and above all and helping her fight their problems, all these months, just like the very first time she was there- for me,...

It had started nearly ten years ago- this- what can one call it? This bond between us.

It was one of the numerous coffee mornings in Moscow. We had just moved there. As was the custom among most expatriates, the ones that had been there for a while, hosted coffees, so the new ones in, could meet some who have been there a bit, and also the other new ones, like us, that moved at the same time.

She had come from Hungary, from Budapest and was full of her time there and even regularly launched into Hungarian, from time to time. Her personality was so very infectious. She spoke with her hands, eyes, her whole body seemed to be in the conversation, following her voice, going high, low and all the rest of it. It was simply fascinating to watch her speak, one didn't even need to nod or make the sounds of agreement from time to time. When she was in flow, it was like a battleship in full charge mode- don't come in her way, and don't even try to interrupt!!

We hit off straightaway. Just like me, she was attractive in her manner and very, very, friendly. We spoke about a great many things and exchanged numbers, amid the coffee and amazing spreads that the hostess, so very kindly, kept us supplied with.

It is strange to explain the connection we have with some people. It's not even as easy as to say it was love at first sight.

It's like a straight dial in and make a soul connection!

I can't put any finger on what actually happened and what she or I really liked about each other or where and on what topic we connected, but we just felt good and comfortable with each other, and that was how it was from the beginning. It was a sort of agreed we are going to be good friends and a mental shake of hands and a hug kind of stuff.

Words seem sort of unnecessary to explain we are, of course, going to keep in touch and so on.

We actually lived a fair distance from each other. Me, in the centre of town in a typical Russian neighbourhood and she, in a gated, expatriate only, community outside the city.

As it happened, with my work and her being busy with two young children, we barely ever met each other. And when we did, it was at dinners hosted by other friends or a birthday party or a festival dinner.

The times we did meet at people's parties, it was getting together for hugely fun and laughter moments and then we were gone our separate ways.

Sort of hard to explain this kind of very personal comfort level we had with each other.

Like the time we were at one who considered herself a society hostesses' festival do, and I casually mentioned to our hostess that I used to sing on the radio in my previous life, and she immediately said, "oh then you must sing for us today".

It was clearly a "I dare you to' kind of - you must sing- as this hostess had adopted a totally patronising tone and look, as if she needed to give the plebeians a chance to let their voice be heard too, and at one of her home shows, no less. I was extremely apprehensive, not only because it was a while since I had done any serious singing, but also because I had seen the obvious challenge in her tone when she asked me to sing. While I hesitated, she, my soul companion, was nearby and said, of course you must sing, you can and I am here with you. She came and sat directly in front of me all the while I sang- the ghazal, a poem that is rendered in a tune with the relevant lines repeated and paused for the audience to absorb, came flowing out, and I sang.

Quite well in fact, going by the applause.

Ranjish hi sahi, dil hi dukhane ke life aa, As phir sae mujhe chod ke jaane ke liye aa.

Kuch to mere pindare muhobbat ka baharam rakh, Tu bhi to kabhi mujhko manane ke liye aa.

Even if it gives my heart more pain and anguish when you leave me again, do come.

Show some respect for my deep love for you, You can come sometimes, to placate me?

And that was that. The evening ended with a nice warm feeling of something well done, and well done with a friend standing by me. What could be better than that?

This is the kind of stuff that made me think it was definitely a soul connection, because I hadn't asked for any help and she never said a single word that sounded like she was helping and yet it was an appeal given and responded to in full measure. Neither of us fell into each others arms or went into a frenzy of thanks or analysing what happened and why and so on.

The sounds in our silence were speaking volumes to

each other. And with complete smoothness of movement.

And we both felt complete, whole and good at the end of it.

There were times we met again, and spent time at dinners and lunches. We always shared many a laugh and chatted about so many things, but we never became close friends in the real sense. We never met regularly or spoke regularly or anything like that. It was hard to find a reason one could put a finger on, and yet, we never managed to move any closer than almost the first time we met, or anywhere near as close to that.

And then we both were moving to a new location, London.

We arrived a few weeks after them. We ended up with homes near each other, a mid sized walk along the same stretch of road. Again we met, and dinners and life continued. This time I was the one with little children while hers were a bit more grown.

Out of the blue a call came from another friend saying do you know, she's very sick with the big C? No I didn't know, and I ended up calling her straightaway and going over in a rush, to see her. Somehow I just had to. I had to see what was happening with her and how the disease was in relation to her. I had to see any marks on her had been made yet, and I had to tell her, to reiterate to her rather, that I was here, for her, day or night, 24/7, in fact.

She looked the same. She was talking to a Swamiji from the Chinmaya Mission and he was telling her to take it calm and slow and conserve her energies for the battle ahead that she now faced.

Hers was a lovely love story that she and her partner were living, high school sweethearts and now life partners and life laid out in terms of a good job and two amazing children. There was so much warmth in their friendship, it was sometimes hard to separate the two. Whoever you spoke to, you got a perfect joint response. That was the amazing thing about it. In this day and age, where could one hope to see such tenderness and such companionship in a relationship? Well, I could see it right here.

The skies had truly erupted over them and the downpour was one that would threaten to wash away everything they had built and nurtured over the years.

She was indeed very very sick. Surgery was done and

then the therapies began. She began to become elusive. Not taking calls and not meeting anyone and not doing any of the things that would bring any sense of normalcy into the days.

Even if I say it was understandable, was it really?

Could I or anyone, even one suffering the same illness, for that matter, actually comprehend what she felt? Even her partner?

It was the uncertainty of it, the ease with which things could just go wrong. Anything could, and at anytime. Not that people don't die from accidents and such, its quite another thing to have your body ravaged by an illness that you have done nothing to contract and yet it chooses you- an illness that can affect every aspect of your life and take from you all that you do and like in your life- like an abusive partner- and yet, you cannot run away from the disease. You cannot hide from it.

You just have to stay there and fight it the best you can. And if that is sufficient you win. If not, you are on your way to losing. Everything. No matter what you feel about it.

All my attempts to keep in touch and keep going over

and offering help were being rebuffed slowly and soon the weeks turned into months and the years seemed to be building up between us too.

As friends, we, the rest of us, kept putting together ideas to set up meetings or small get togethers. Small ones and of only the closest of friends, so she would feel secure enough to visit and once in a while, we were successful. It was heart wrenching to hear her speak of not knowing how to plan beyond a week or two at best as she didn't know what was going to happen.

It couldn't be anything one would ever wish for, to sit next to your friend describe why she didn't want to meet anyone anymore. She said, its hard for me to listen to people describe their life and the things they are doing and are planning to do, whereas I am not allowed to have any plan for my life or my family's. I have to be in readiness for the disease always. There's no saying when it will take the upper hand and all our lives only revolve around that. I can be demanding and insist on having my family and friends around me at all times, but that's it. They still cannot comprehend the sinking that's happening with me, feeling myself going deeper into this dark black hole where every moment seems to be a more clear indication that I'm crossing the boundaries into the point of no return.

What could one have done to be generously swamped with a disease like the big "C"? What indeed?

The feelings of self pity or self deprecation are so raw in her voice, I can sense it in the air around her. Loud and clear. How can she help feeling sorry for herself, I wonder.

I have always had very strong intuitive strength which has stood me in excellently good stead all through my life. If anything, it has become a well honed and fine tuned ability I now possess and am able to take heed of, over the years. Thinking calmly and repetitively about anything or any incident, usually presents to me, the cause, why it happened and the possible solution, or the way around it too. I am used to going into deep meditation as well, given the stresses I have been in many a time. And over the years, I became completely in tune with my energies and the energies around me, the positive as well as the negative ones.

I believe in the universal energy and in the energies in all of nature around me. The seamlessness with which it flows all around me. The vastness of it. The power of the energy in everything around me and the oneness that I feel with it are very powerful feelings in me. I feel like a complete and inseparable part of it. It is an extremely liberating feeling as well. Being one with nature. I also became very sensitive to recognising negative energies too and wherever possible warned people about their presence. My meditation is sometimes so powerful, I begin to have out of body experiences. I begin to sense energies in people that were away in another part of the city I live in, or even halfway across the world, in another country sometimes and very precisely so. I know what they are thinking and what is needed to be done to change it. If someone was feeling the threat of being overwhelmed by emotion or if someone was reaching out to me- one can't get more pure that that kind of energy passing between people.

Time went on and it was now nearly ten years since

she was first diagnosed. She continued to be reclusive, not answer messages or respond to calls easily. But I kept at it. I kept sending her messages on her whatsapp chat, a new tool that allowed us to be in touch and see if the other has seen our messages. Presto! It was several steps above leaving voice messages or emails even.

Another friend was planning to having mediation sessions at her home with Sandy, a very good guru to follow for meditation. We, her friends, felt it would be good for her to get some positive energies going rather than let the dark black ones cloud over her, bogging her down into a sense of fear and depression she didn't have the energy to fight nor needed to be in.

To convince her to come and try it out, we both went over to hers and spent some time. It was a rare occasion that she decided to call us over to her place. There she gave us one of her fabulous lunches and after that, on her request, I sang for her too- the positive energy from my meditation flowed through my music and was palpable by the end of the song. The three of us were encased in the positivity and sat there in a complete harmony.

We managed to convince her to try and attend the meditation sessions with no strings attached. I would pick her up and drive her- I did the honours. I went picked up and took my soulmate along with me for the sessions. This went on for a couple of times.

The meditation sessions themselves were horrible for me too. She said they were bad and charged with negativity for her. For my part, the sheer force of the negative energy and the thick black clouds that threatened to swallow me were so intense, I always snapped out of the mediation, very shaken indeed. I felt I needed to move away from the room quickly. I spoke about it at length, to the instructor, Sandy and he said, it happens when someone around me had some deep worry in their heart. We both knew she did.

I tried my best to talk to her to let go fo the fear. To let the feelings flow freely over her and that way they would flow out of her, but she was was too fearful. She was so afraid of what was going to happen. What she thought was going to happen, that is. And we fought a lost cause. She refused to come to any more sessions and nothing we said could persuade her to change her mind. She was back in her home. In her shell. She didn't want to meet anymore.

That was it. In two months from that date she was gone.

It was almost fortuitous that I met her one last time too. I kept getting these reaching outs for help, for me to hold her mentally and support her, and kept calling her, but she couldn't come to the phone and I couldn't go either. One morning I was going to the meditation session and having been to the temple recently, I was holding on to some of the offering I had brought back with me, to give to her. I just drove over on the way and stopped at her place. I knocked the door and her Mother opened. I gave her the offering and said please make sure she gets it. Her Mother asked me to wait and said she wants to see you. I went in. There she was. Sitting in the chair. So frail, I was afraid to go near or touch her for fear of hurting her by accident. I sat on the floor near her and spoke to her for a while. She was just back from the hospital and the prognosis was not good. It was a matter of time as the medication was getting too strong for her to take in, and if she didn't have the medication, the disease was spreading in her. Either way the time she had left was just like that in the little hourglass and the sand was perfectly and slowly trickling her life away. We could but watch. Against all my intuition that was repeatedly telling me she is losing this battle, I reassured her the best I could.

Her agony as she struggled those last days were palpable for me. I sensed her restlessness so much, I tried to call as often as I could without seeming rude, but her relative, who had never met me, decided in her own wisdom, to not let me speak to her. Perhaps she felt there was no point in wasting her energy with someone who wasn't perhaps close even. Her relative just said she can't speak now. I could hardly explain to her how many messages I was getting from her and how intense they were in their urgency, asking, no, demanding I get in touch and immediately.

I was at my wits end how to calm myself and control all these surging currents of intense emotional appeals coming thick and fast. It was all a new one for me too. I couldn't get enough respite from meditating a lot either. I was tense and disturbed all the time and it was affecting my days a lot.

I sent many messages to her and as always got no response. She seemed to see them, I thought, looking at the blue ticks instead of black ones, but something didn't seem right. It just did not add up. I was beginning to feel I was on the death watch. Reluctantly on one hand but unable to let go on the other, I braced myself for the inevitable news to come.

And come it did. Surely and uncompromising in its finality. She had gone. Just like that. Was that the end, I wondered.

It wasn't. I woke up the next day to a desperate urgency to go to her home and see her husband and children. Again, just like that. We were friends and all that but to intrude on his or their grief seemed presumptuous, but I could do nothing to even think I won't go now!

I just took my partner along and there I was, ringing on her doorbell. Her husband answered and wordlessly I just went forward and hugged him. It seemed to me that I was doing these actions but someone else was directing them.

I shook off the feeling thinking I was wanting to condole him too and offer any help as well at this time. Her sister came and asked for some help with tableware and I offered to bring over some food too. Which I did.

The days passed and the funeral ceremony was held and we all attended it. It was hard to go through it but again I felt I was lending my eyes for someone else to follow the proceedings. Try as I might, the feeling only grew stronger. Like after the funeral, when I saw her Mother across the garden, on some volition, certainly not my own, as I would think twice before intruding again on her private grief, I raced across the lawn to her and spent time talking to her. She wanted her hand to be held by me and for me to lead her to the entrance, to the car, and I just went along with that. The car came along and I helped her into it.

A strange feeling came over me. I couldn't go to her home again, surely?

We had been invited to her home for a party that evening and we went along. I was like someone in a trance. I was going around, seeing people and speaking to them but it felt like I was wanting to just observe what was going on, not participate really.

I stayed as long I could but the feeling of doing things not of my own volition or instinct was very strong, and I left.

The days that followed kept me thinking of her home, her husband and her son particularly. By now I could see her in front of me and near me, asking me to check on him and do this or that. I was under the impression that my own intense energy surges around the time of her passing were telling on my nerves and it was perhaps just the aftershock that I was experiencing and nothing more. After all, seeing a person after they pass on is something close relatives, spouses, siblings or children seem to be doing. Not me, I thought. It didn't seem right. How was it even possible? In this day and age. I wasn't a close friend either, inspire of our immense soul connection that has stood for so many years. Even with my deep belief in my mediation and soul energy and the universal energy even, I found it hard to accept these post death appearances in my life. Why me, that too was something I would like answered. Why bother with me, a person on the outside perhaps when a person in the inner circle, whether a friend or a relative, would be a safer bet?

It was intrusive even at times when she would appear and say do this or go to my place or check how my son is and have you been helping properly. At other times it would be like drop whatever you are doing anyway, since my home and my family are much more important and everything else comes a distant second, if that.

When I say do this, I expect you to do it, and jump to it, she seemed to say.

This went on for a while and soon I found her getting more and more aggressive about it. Even when I was calm, helpful and understanding or when I tried to tell her that this was all I could do at the moment or that I just couldn't really turn up at her place every time a hat dropped or whatever the saying was. I found her flashing her eyes and tossing her head to say no, you do this now.

And one day things came to a head. I was already feeling the strain of someone being around me and being so restless as well that I was feeling constantly on edge. I had become irritable, short of sleep and was tiring under the constant prodding.

It wasn't like I was not keeping in touch or not helping as much as I could. I did and would continue fo do so. But that was not good enough a response.

She said, with wild kind of laugh and toss of her head and in a menacing tone, if you don't want to go to my place or do these things I am asking you to do, I will go to your children. I will get into their heads and mess them up. And that flashed a bright red in front of my eyes. Like are rag to a bull, I lifted my head and was completely furious as I told her not to even think of trying that. I said it in as warning a tone as I dared, but I got a sinking feeling inside. What had I let myself in for. What was I doing listening to voices from the grave that were trying to scare me and now seemed to be succeeding? Who would believe that? Such a tall story! Mostly they would say I needed to perhaps rest from overwork or that

I needed to cut out my meditation for a while as it seemed to be giving me so many fanciful ideas about spirits and all the fairyland kind of stuff!

I did try to be stern and strong and forceful when I warned her, and she seemed to back down at the time, but what guarantees did I have? Nothing at all. No way to ensure she didn't go near my children or didn't try any stunts with them. What could I do to protect them from her?

I was virtually losing my head now. Try as I might she was invading my head and I could not even meditate to bring in some calm for myself. She seemed to be right there inside my head and trying to take control of me. I felt that so strongly, I couldn't keep my eyes shut anymore and snapped out of it. What now? What was I going to do?

I could relate to her instinctive need to solve her family's problems and make their lives smoother and happier, if she could. As a mother and wife I did understand this attachment and affection that made me continually almost be there, just be there for my family. But I could not appreciate nor condone this at-the-point-of-a-knife kind of insistence or however remote, though in this case quite explicitly put, threats. I definitely drew the line there.

I, rather we, was or were connected truly, I think. We had the mutual understanding and bond that was felt strongly on both sides, and not only felt, we each reached out whenever we felt the pull and acted in the manner needed to help the other, with the most minimum of fuss. In fact, we never even mentioned this in the way of conversation either. Such, I thought, was the nature of our relationship and yet it seemed to be ready to be marred by this seemingly wilful, aggression.

Here I was trying to get my head around this new situation in my life, where I seemed to be overwhelmed with increasingly dangerous messages from the 'other world" and a spirit of someone I considered to be my soulmate, that seemed to have now turned renegade and was threatening to invade my brain and take control of me, when I was invited to a dinner party at a close friend's place. And like manna from heaven, Sandy, the meditation guru, appeared to be there at the dinner too. I had to ask him what was going on. Was I just plain imagining things or was any of this for real. How real was this threat I was under. How could anyone possibly be so connected to a person or persons who were friends or relatives but not that close as to be eating-from-the same-plate or sleeping-in-the-same-bed kind of close. It was something counterintuitive, was it not. One could hardly turn on one's receptiveness like a radio receiver and become the recipient of local or non-local S.O.S. signals for help!! Really!!Even with my deep mediative reflections, out of body experiences, I was still not entirely convinced. Maybe it was my fears coming to the fore.

He listened to me and when I finished he asked if I had called out to her at all. Did I reach out to her in any way or encourage her at all. I said no. He then said that in times of need or distress, a human's soul reaches out or cries out for help. The cries can be heard clearly and absorbed by pure souls around who have loads of positive energy in them.

So the good news is that I am a pure soul with loads of positive energy. What could I do with that. I was shaking my head with mixed emotions. It therefore, so happened that my soulmate's cries for help were heard by me and I was responding to her need. The fact that she was not backing off when I had actually gone and visited her place or done her family the help they needed at the time, seemed to suggest she was trying to influence me more.

He taught me a way to protect my energy from such negative forces. The first steps in mediation were to recognise your powers of perception and intuitive thinking and positive energy. Then I needed to learn to harness them so as to be able to push away or keep away or even turn away any negative energies that threaten to overwhelm me at any time. By doing this, I could turn her away from me and that way her negativity wouldn't spread over me either.

Energy was energy, to put it simply. The positive and the negative are all around us. Just as we react to someone we've just met thinking, Oh, perhaps I don't really like this person much- without even a single word exchanged. Its just the energies reaching out and touching each other and not liking what they experience. That makes us sometimes move away from people even on initial contact, while it may be true that they are the right sort of person for us to interact with, even if they have a strong defence mechanism that seems to repel us. So while initial instincts about people, like animal instincts are very useful to acknowledge and really correct too, one also needs to prepare for this sort of situation where things have gone out of hand. Once the soul has left the body, so to speak, there isn't much it can achieve in terms of helping the loved ones, and that can lead to some desperation. But threats, even ones caused by anguish or helplessness are still threats, and need to be recognised for what they are first of all, and then defused quickly permanently, before they cause any harm to anyone. That cannot be a solution to frustrated anxiety. My thoughts seemed to arrange themselves in the logical order I was used to and I was humbly grateful.

I was much obliged for the advice and upon following his instruction, soon able to becalm myself again.

Things kept moving and life went on as well. Soon days made months, few at first and then many, and we were at the turn of the year. The first anniversary of her passing.

There was a prayer organised at the local community hall. I was going to attend. As I drove there I suddenly found her travelling with me. Clearly she intended to come to the ceremony too.

She came with me. Just as she's been with me for over a year now. She came into the hall and as I stopped and looked around, so did she. We were among the first to arrive. Only her family was there. As I stood for a moment to debate where I should sit, I felt the gentle push towards her family. I greeted them and went to sit on the carpet just behind them but a little distance between us. The prayers began and the singers were mesmerising in their rendering of the chosen devotional hymns. It seemed she had chosen the hymns herself. She was one with the song. We swayed with the devotion that poured from every one of them. I saw myself even begin to dance in bliss. She was on her feet, moving and swaying with the music. Every nuance she took in, and revelled. She blessed her lovely children and swept around her family and friends!!!

She was so very happy to see everyone.

For so long, a full year now, she has been with me and worried daily, about her home, her family. I felt each moment of her restlessness. The agony, the fear, the worry what would happen...

Every time I did my best reassure her it would be alright and that she should not worry like this.

This time it was different!! This time she was content! She was happy! She came towards me and with joy in her heart and a huge smile on her face, she was saying thank you to me... crazy girl....for staying at her side, for enduring each of her fears, for helping her fight them, deal with them, overcome them, all these months, together, just like the very first time she helped me do the same, all those days ago, at the dinner party.

I could never have imagined I would be so far away from her in real life, and yet, be such a close and intertwined part of her life. I could never have imagined our journey together would take us through so many new paths. My head was bowed as I paused to think of what she and I have been through. It started well before she was a free spirit. But it was now the time to celebrate.

Her liberation. Her freedom. From the bonds of this life however full it may have been.

She's truly free in spirit now. Her journey is different. She is truly at peace now, and so am I.

The Yen of Happiness

Raat yun dil me teri khoyi hui yaad aaye, Jaise veerane me chupke se bahaaar aa jaaye

Jaise sehera me haule se chale baad e naseeb, Jaise beemar ko be vajaha karaar, aa jaaye!

Last night your faded memory came to me; As in the wilderness spring comes quietly,

As, slowly, in the desert, moves the breeze; As, to a sick man, without cause, comes peace!

It was Tuesday morning. 8 am. Sailesh swiped himself into the treasury floor at the bank. It was going to be exciting to see what happened to the yen after yesterday's edgy finish. He took his seat at the treasury traders desk and looked around. Everyone was gearing up for the days dealings.

There was always a very high level of understated anticipation here. As if everyone was waiting to see what the currencies did. Every single day. And they didn't disappoint.

Sailesh blinked.

For a moment he was still at the cafe downstairs. He struggled to get his mind to the present. He had to. The market was opening any minute now, and every second counted, here on the treasury trading floor. Every hundredth of a second sometimes.

But today the scene he had gone through kept pulling him back. He was forced to relive it. He stopped fighting and let it go on to play mode in his mind.

He had picked up his coffee at the self service and was moving to the cashier and there she was, sitting in a corner table and working on her laptop. She looked up at him as he passed and he was lost. He froze. Here he was, the great hot-shot trader. He could handle blip like movements in the currencies without a split breath even. Forget turning a hair or any such. The treasury floor stretched for miles almost, two football fields side by side in length and endless rows of the traders and all the support staff. The treasury trading room itself was this really quiet circular room with its tables and multiple screens blinking out currency rates, exchanges, availabilities, trades and also news and all the other information he needed to watch all the time he was trading.

He couldn't afford to miss any of it. Things could get really ugly in half a heartbeat. He was well known and famous all over the treasury trading floors for keeping so beautifully cool, under the enormous pressure during trading. He was also a seasoned player here. Someone who took amazingly calculated risks in his trades seamlessly. And made huge monies for the bank in the process. He was a star, not on the ascendent, but fully risen and firmly on the bright sky of success. People looked at him all the time trying to read his expressions and match their trading with it. Or use his supposed reaction as information for their own trading. But he was so savvy at keeping a deadpan expression.

Here, at the cafe, though, he was lost. Sailesh was sure his tongue was in knots. He could not think of a single thing he could say to her. But why would he want to speak to her at all? What is this irresistible urge to find out more, if not all, about her? What set his heart all into a flutter?

She was really ever so lovely. No question about that. And very smartly turned out too. Subtly elegant and perfectly fitting into, he thought, in this part of the bank. He felt himself being pulled like a line being reined in. His feet just couldn't help but walk in her direction. Should he say hello? Or something about the weather, being as they were, in all weather impressive London??

He stood still for several moments and lost in thinking those "don't know what thoughts," until the person behind tapped him on his shoulder and said wryly, I think you should move up!!

He looked at the girl again and moved on.

That was few weeks ago.

The traders were gearing up for something big again. It happened every ever so once in a while. The market decided to spice things up. Every one was hooked to the yen- it had gained almost 200 pips in the past four trading sessions and the word in the market was that there would be a news to bring it another 100 higher.

These sort of days were Sailesh's favourite ones. The superb adrenaline rush that came with the markets opening and all the overnight trading positions settling in. It felt so much like a passionate love affair unfolding slowly, layer by layer, in front of him. Just being on this forex trading floor gave him a comfortable, totally at home feeling at worst, and all the heart-thumping excitement of a wild roller coaster ride on his best days.

And when he caught the currency swing correctly, he could hardly contain his excitement to see where it all lead up to. That's what he lived for most days. Most days he woke, walked, ate, drove, thought and to be totally fair, even smelt currencies and forex markets.

He had always liked numbers. His mother said he could count before he said his first regular word like "mom". And from there it was up, up and away.

Numbers spoke to him, gave him patterns, told him stories, even when he brushed his teeth it was for billions of nanoseconds and not for the two minutes that dentists quoted.

He counted his walking and even his words. His favourite words were ones with most alphabets, a mile long, with prime numbers of alphabets and every other mathematical way of describing the English words.

He always explained reactions in percentages of feeling, and distances or time down to the metre or microsecond. It was never 60 per cent. It was indeed 60.23 per cent!

He excelled in writing stories with distances, speeds, accelerations, falls, drops - all quantitative data, in short.

It was to be expected he would move on to physics, quantum physics. The devil was always in the detail. The how and why was so fascinating, he had double graduated at the top of his class before he wanted to pause and take a breather even.

He had been on this floor for three years now. Some of his friends, who joined with him, just quit soon after, saying it was too quick and way too stressful. Some stayed, so there was a healthy camaraderie between them, though he was ahead by a few lengths. Not that he wore it on his sleeve. He was a very likeable sort of chap with a winning smile when he chose to part with the deadpan expression he wore normally.

He absolutely revelled in the adrenalin rush trading gave him. The excitement of bidding at the speed of a split seconds and for pips, essentially hundredths of percentage points, was totally fascinating. It was like going deep into a teeny, tiny part of a currency and making a whole world out there, trading the smallest fraction of its value.

And making profit, super alpha profits, when he got it right. That was satisfying too. Getting it right was the big drug that drove him, rather than the money.

The next time he went to the cafeteria he looked the place over just in case, and there she was. This time the suit was a kind of beige with green. Of course he thought she looked fantastic. She seemed to sense his glance and looked up- their gaze met and they both sort of smiled, and immediately looked away. What on earth was he doing?? Smiling at a stranger like that? And what would she think? That he was some sort of type, trying the smile as a conversation opener?? A pick up type??

He rushed out of the cafeteria. If he had bothered to look around he would have seen her get up and start towards him.

There went the bell. Start of trading. He had recently been given a higher leverage to trade with so he had more "cash" to play around with. He promptly placed a 100,000 on the yen rising 40 pips and the euro was looking ready for a nudge too. And on it went until the bell. And like a balloon, he could feel the air of excitement leave him. Until tomorrow then, he thought as he got up, collected his things and moved to his desk, to enter every trade into the system. So that the back office could calculate all his open positions and evaluate what his risk position overnight was.

Japan would be opening in a few hours, so, well before he came back to his seat on the floor, the yen would have done its bit of a jig or jog already.

He felt someone touch his elbow in the queue. He turned mouthing an apology, only to find, it was "the girl". "I am sorry to startle you, she said, but I wanted to speak to you. May I?"

"Yes of course", he said. "I'll just bring my drink".

She stepped back toward the seat she was sitting on. He picked up his fresh green smoothie with ginger- this was his latest fascination. A drink with lemon, green mango, spinach, cucumber, and ginger. It tasted just wow. And he was hooked.

Sailesh sat down opposite her.

"First things first," she said. "Hi, I am Amy Kamath".

"I am Sailesh Sundar," he replied. "Very nice to meet you".

"Yes, and to meet you too", Amy said. "I've been wanting to talk to you for ages. Though you always come in, you always seem to be in a hurry. And look totally lost. So I hadn't the heart to intrude for ages."

Oh my dear God, he thought. What on earth is going on? She had been trying to talk to him? Yes, she had smiled at him once-

What a mess. It's all this new age "my space and no one is to invade it" nonsense they drill into us that makes us this confused, he thought, his mind racing.

They tell us to be kind and helpful to strangers but

never to speak to them. They tell us to be part of our surroundings and society but never to interact with unknown women- who knows who may be a man eater?? Really? Maneaters among us. That is what it has come down to.

All this idea that girls and boys, once they grow up are always looking for a mate rubbish- just makes for absolutely abnormal, stiff necked and very paranoid bunch of youth, out of totally nice and simple people.

Sailesh shrugged his mind, shook it a little to snap out of these thoughts. She was waiting. Amy, she said her name was.

He pulled up out the chair next to hers and sat down.

"Don't you think it is all a bit weird to have us so inhibited from even speaking to other people nowadays," she asked.

"Wow, mindreader,' he thought.

"Hi, I'm Sailesh. Currency trader for a living and looking for a friend in the rest of my life. Nice to meet you, Amy. What brings you to the BIT?"

"I am doing a project here for a few weeks and since

I am from Cardiff, and I don't know many people in London, I am having a bit of a hard time."

"Oh, sorry to hear that," Sailesh ventured, feeling his body begin to relax even more at this bit of news." I know the feeling of being new in a place and the only people you speak to are at your workplace so that doesn't help at all does it?"

"Yes that is just it, since I am not here for long, it seems odd to even make friends but what else can I do with myself," Amy seemed to ask herself and him at the same time.

"I am on a project. Kind of marketing project. I am to study how a person might react to a new situation."

Hearing this Sailesh was struck dumb for a moment. All his interests from the beginning were mathematical, in physics or now into currencies. He rarely read or spoke about anything else, save the occasional music concerts he went to, or some music he had listened to. That was pretty much the range of his conversation skills. He could go length and breadth as well as deep, as deep as you liked, into these, but he had practically close to nothing to talk about marketing, the psychology of it, and even less about a project in or exploring or the mind of any other person.

Still he was feeling super brave that day when he began to ask her questions about her work.

His mind was quietly racing around his memory bank, trying to find any nuggets he had stored away on any marketing ideas or news that he had read recently,

It was very unusual for him to go forward and continue this sort of conversation. It had never happened in the past, ever. The moment anyone, male or female, had interests that he didn't, Sailesh would wind down into first, a silence and then with a short excuse made, he was up and away from the person, never to return again. For some reason, this was always the modus operandi and it suited him really well too.

So far at least. But today was different. Seemed a day to make new tracks. Well, he was very ill equipped to speak to Amy, was he not, he thought, mentally kicking himself for not paying more attention to broadening his range of subjects, when he was reading.

All was lost, or was it? For one, he did not feel

like giving up. Something seemed to have a grip in the small of his back and was keeping him in position, constantly prodding him to pay attention. To continue the conversation. This lovely lady, Amy, seemed to have something that pulled at him.

He, for one, had the habit of conversing with people only on topics he understood and followed, and not ever when he could only listen and not participate. Not for him the "wing it and see what happens" some were prone to indulge in. And it certainly would not do the trick- not with someone he was trying to break a friendship barrier. At the very least. Somehow he felt he was feeling those violins in his head telling him these were the magical moment he was waiting for.

He did remember some of his fellow classmates at business school talk of marketing principles, the discussions they had- they used to get all excited about why a new product was a good one and why they were sure it would fail! Seemed counterintuitive to him at the time. Still did. Why on earth would a good product fail? Did people not know a good thing when they saw it? In all his time in financial services, he did not know of a good product that had failed. He knew, for a fact, many bad ones that were successful for a while, due to amazing packaging and marketing by the banks that designed them, until the regulators got their act together and plugged that particular loophole as well.

Sometimes the product was designed to counter or go around the particular legal framework. What his bosses would call 'stretching the law', but not breaking it. And making a huge green pile in the process. Those kind of need based products, he too, had successfully designed in the early days of his career, when he was trying out selling equity stocks.

The government allowed foreign institutions to purchase local company shares only in the secondary market, meaning only via stock exchanges. And there were many companies which did not want to go through the stock market route to raise money. Either they were happy with the numbers of public holding their shares or they did not want to take up the expense of making a public offering of their shares, being medium or small sized themselves. Public offerings meant lot of regulatory compliances as well because the stringent requirements of the various bodies to file documents making the needed disclosures, filed in a timely manner. It was risky as well, since it could well happen that enough numbers of public would not be interested in buying their shares.

All in all, there was a problem. Sailesh came up with a product that allowed the companies to access investment from their chosen foreign institutions, meaning those they felt they could work with, and at the same time met the regulatory requirements without breaking any of the laws that governed the securities markets.

But that was securities. This was marketing and not even to do with currency markets.

He brought out his phone and began to idly flick through his contacts making mental asterisks on the marketing lot.

He went on to the search engine and began to play with the words marketing, psychology of buyers, principles of marketing, strategy and so on.

The web, being the magnificent beast it was, began to

throw out multitudes of reams of intricate, as well as deep, research papers of data towards him. Man, he thought, I'm drowning in it already.

Will I be able to sink, surface and swim in this information, reach a stage of keeping on top of this and get to the level of understanding any jargon Amy may use and make pithy remarks of my own?

He almost reached for his belt to tighten it. Go for it pal, his mind seemed to urge him. You can do this. You are going to do it!

And so it began. Their daily meetings at the coffee shop became a ritual which both of them were eager to go through, not missing a single day. At first it was hesitant conversations and then long discussions on several aspects of marketing, market research and the psychology of the buyer. They seemed to lose track of time.

Sailesh's evenings were organised into a quick meal, the best being the ready to heat and eat variety, and settling into the topic of the day. He progressed from five Ps to the more complex seven Ps, from identifying a product to creating a market to understanding the mind of a seller to creating an image in the mind of a buyer. If one day the urgency was to analyze market opportunities, the next day could be a task on how to select target markets. The intricacies of designing marketing strategies were unfolding over a stuffed baguette lunch while the planning of marketing programmes, organising, implementing and controlling the marketing effort went over several days of breakfast bagel and coffee.

Very quickly Amy and Sailesh realised the short time they shared before the work day and on occasion, at lunch time, were simply not enough. They needed to see each other more and for more time, without having a job to go to or any deadline to meet. It wasn't just the that they liked each other. Or that they just seemed to be eager to share their ideas and listen to the other. They genuinely seemed like they were building something here. A bond that was drawing them close like the threads of a web, weaving around them while they chatted away. There was no question of not meeting or saying they couldn't. Each seemed to move all other things to do or engagements to keep, away from their calendar and leave all the time in the world for each other. Wasn't this the best way to give time to a new relationship and see how that panned out. To nurture the little seed of contact that had come their way so it could take root and put forth little shoots with tiny leaves. It was theirs to build and theirs to build in a way that the two of them wanted.

The days passed full of 'in a kind of light as a feather moments'. Both of them were indeed floating on air. Their manner was not engaging in anything else they did, when they were not together that is. Their rest of the life was routine that was simply dealt with. They began to rush through every single action, much to the surprise of their friends, especially since neither was prone to being inattentive at all.

Life was chugging along beautifully it would seem. From marketing they moved to psychology and sure enough Freud and his views on dream came and went over dinners shared and beautiful sunsets which may have felt hurt, if they had feelings, for putting out their displays of sometimes brilliant and sometimes subtle colours, which clearly, were wasted on our young twosome.

As days moved into weeks, even Jack Trout and Al Reis made an entry. The complications of positioning were mulled over. Sailesh's new found knowledge in his personal night school was being put to good use. He could confidently say that Positioning is not about creating something new and different. It's about manipulating what's already in the prospect's mind. It's about bridging the connections that already exist. The mind usually screens and rejects much of the information offered and accepts only that which matches prior knowledge or experience. And once it is made up, it is almost impossible to change the mind. The best approach to take in would be to present a message that is very simple. Wow!

What a huge world was out there and he only just got to know it.

And there was another world that was being nurtured too. The way Amy walked along and how she looked for him as she came closer, how her pace changed when she saw him. Her face was always a 'ready to break into a smile' kind of one, but the smile beginning and spreading across her face, seemed to light something up inside him, giving him a great thrill, so he was several feet in the air. Most days Amy would come close and give him a silent 'what are you looking at' look, and he would shake his head and begin to talk about whatever it was they were discussing.

He did notice that they never spoke to each other about anything other than what was relevant to marketing or the psychology of it. They never spoke of their own lives, except a distant reference to where they grew up or where they studied. Where they travelled to maybe, on occasion. But never anything their own. Nothing of their likes, dislikes, their feelings. That was it. They never spoke of how they felt, in all this time. Why, he wondered. Wasn't it natural for people to talk about their feelings too. Why hide them? No, hide was the wrong word. Why skirt around them, every time? What was this hesitancy to speak of themselves? They both seemed to indulge in it.

Sailesh was not sure how this was going. They both were very happy to meet and spend hours. His friends would be halfway up to the altar in this time, he knew. Then what was it? Should he try to broach a different subject? Should he try today? Every day seemed to come and go with him not taking the step.

Four months had passed. It was time to make the move, Sailesh decided. Today. I'll do it. He dressed and walked to the dinner date with a sense of purpose. No holding back today. The setting was perfect. On the banks of the river, under the trees, tables set at a comfortable distance from each other so no eavesdropping was possible- perfect setting!

Well, this is it, he thought. I must speak about my feelings and see if the signs I have been seeing are the right ones or not. Sailesh lingered on that thought for a moment. Perhaps he was still unsure if he was really reading the signs right and Amy too was as comfortable in his company as he felt. Thats why he kept putting this conversation off for the next day and the next. But, as in the timeless tradition, it cannot go on like this.

Amy arrived on time and he saw her get out hurriedly out of the taxi and walk towards him. There was the eagerness he knew and felt in himself too. The sudden leap his heart took and then felt all restless and impatient. The rush his mind went in way ahead and almost embraced Amy, while his body stood still. They greeted each other and almost in unison said, 'I've got something to tell you'.

Amy was very keen to go first. So Sailesh waited for her to speak.

'I'll tell you as quickly as I can, Sailesh. I have come to the end of my stay here. I will be returning to my home town in the next couple of days. It was essential for me to stay here to complete this project I was working on, which is an essential part of my doctorate studies in psychology.'

'Where did this come from? What do you mean you are moving back? And what has it got to do with us? There is an us, isn't there?, Sailesh blurted out, with so much feeling Amy just looked at him. She looked a bit upset too today, he just seemed to notice.

'I know it all seems very sudden and I did, I do like your company, Sailesh, but I only got to know you to complete my project. I know it sounds selfish and unfeeling. I was chosen to do this project by your company. Since I was

113

going to do this research as part of my doctoral studies, your company had approached my university to sponsor two of us. You know how expensive it can be to go out and do this kind of long study. They chose me to do it here, and for their sponsorship, I am supposed to share the report with them. I was okay with that and so I was given a list of three people, by your company, whom I could approach and spend time with, to get the information for my study. If things didn't go well between us, I would have had to contact the next person on this list. But a great big thanks to you, I've had a wonderful time as well and got all the material I need for my report. You made these past days easy and truly as wonderful as could be. Who does that for someone they are barely getting to know?

I am sure this may sound selfish to you, Sailesh, me saying goodbye like this, but for what it is worth, I genuinely like you and really enjoyed our time together. You are a wonderful person and all your innocence, and, in spite of being so very successful at your work, the curiosity you show for new things, all the effort you made to talk to me about marketing or the psychology of it-perhaps you have been spending long nights reading up!'

'Dear Lord,' he thought, 'she was on to that!! How utterly embarrassing'. Sailesh felt himself grow all hot and uncomfortable.

While he was stunned to begin with, he slowly began to relax. There was nothing offensive in her manner, not earlier, and not now. She seemed as caring and he felt the same. They were both still comfortable with each other.

'I am not sure what I should say, Amy,' Sailesh said slowly. 'Shall we have dinner together and spend this evening as we had planned? We can then say goodbye?'

They both sat down to the meal. It was delicious and while they talked the gorgeous sunset was taking place in front of them. They talked about the many things like they always did, they they met. The companionable chat between them was just as enthusiastic as it had been all these past days. They both were eager to put their points of view across, and, just as eager to listen to the other's point of view.

'Take care', they said to each other, with a lot feeling. 'Stay well'.

The next morning came along and there he was, getting his coffee.

All this had been a study in how to make friends, in the modern context, and, was simply the part of a psychology doctoral studies, to become a psychiatrist? Sponsored by his bank? Which was why she was allowed to come here into the cafe inside the bank, so often?

He put on his coat adjusted his collar and tied the belt buckle. With a quick movement he picked up his bag, slung his over his shoulder, picked up his coffee cup, and, glancing over his shoulder to check he hadn't left anything behind, walked out of the door, into the world outside.

Oh my goodness!! The skies had opened out into a huge downpour in the time he was having this conversation with himself.

He stopped for a moment and turned his face to the sky. The rain came quick and fast onto his face, streaming loads of cool water, seemingly relentlessly. He stood still. Then he smiled. If he had been had, so totally and royally, why not have a dousing, a drubbing and a full drenching too, while he was at it. The skies would love that too!

Well, to be fair, it was he who had all the thoughts on making a romance of this friendship, and not one from Amy. That much he gave credit for. It was time to walk on.

The way forward and the daily swings of the Yen, beckoned. This was familiar turf, yeah! He could do this, right? He took a sip of his coffee and as if on cue, the phone began to buzz with the pre-market opening updates.

Restart

Kuch is tarah maine zindagi ko asaan kar diya, kisi se maafi maang li, kisi ko maaf kar diya!

I made my life easier in this way, some people I asked for forgiveness and some, I forgave!

It was the routine for the past few weeks now. It was dark outside again. It wasn't the usual cloudy and grey skies that had become the usual view from the window before bedtime. In the pitch black night sky, the stars seemed to be twinkling again, high in the sky. They were her friends.

Every night her Mum, Suha and her Dad, Sri, came upstairs to check how she and her brother brushed their teeth and then tucked them both into their beds. Most days Dad made up a story about her favourite dragon and when that story ended, Mum read a story or told Angel a story she knew. Angel and her brother, Henry, took turns to choose the book for the story sessions. Meticulous records were kept of who chose what and when. No deviations were permitted and many a tantrum lurked close to the surface at those moments, where a possible misdirected choice was even debatably possible to maybe have been likely to be entered into. There was always also a side, running score kept in case they had swapped days or been generous and traded in their day for a future day.

Every night Angel thought she too would fall asleep like her brother. He fell asleep the moment he climbed into his bed and his head touched the pillow. Gone before you could say the magic word even!

And every night, after Mum and Dad tucked her into bed, Angel spent her nights looking at the sky from her window. She had a lovely room, it was at the top of the house. It was big and airy, and had a neat play room attached to it. The windows were sloping so she could lie in bed and look out at the sky.

It was a beautifully done room, light blue walls and the night sky on the ceiling. Mum had attached glow stickers of fairies and planets to the ceiling, so it seemed, for a long while after lights out, that the sky had come in, with the little glowing stars. The walls had pictures from her travels. The pattern was so much like a real night sky. And her night lamp was a bunch of sea creatures reflecting on a surface that rotated with the warmth of the light.

And the view as quite hypnotic. Anyone could and would fall asleep watching that.

She sat up. The bed was too small again. No, that was not quite right. The bed was a good size, bigger than her brother's, but not big enough when you looked at all the toys she would pack into bed with her each night.

Toys of every shape and size - the big green crocodile she had bought on the trip to the zoo. The fifteen odd spider men she had in her collection... ones that flew, wove webs, walked, talked, twinkled with lights, in fact she had most of the options available in the market.

And with all that company even, sleep would not come to her. The sleep she craved. The sleep she so desperately wanted. The lovely sleep where she would dream of riding the horses and slaying dragons. The dreams where she would go off on a big boat with her telescope and explore the high seas. Where she would scan the oceans for each type of fish, big and small that she knew. For each type of sea creature she had read about in her sea life book. That sea life book was her lifeline. She knew every animal, big or small, that walked the surface of the ocean, rather swam or lived in the oceans. She knew what they were like, what they ate and where they could be found. The film on the deepest point in the ocean was one of her favourites.

The beautiful restful sleep that she so so knew from her childhood- her childhood? That was a funny thought though for someone who was the ripe old age of, well, she was all of six years old now!!

Angel had spent nights looking at the sky for a few weeks now.

Today she felt more lost and upset than usual. She got off the bed and went down the stairs to where her parents room was. Like every day she stopped on the landing. Should she wake them or not?

She just sat down on the last step silently.

Suha, her Mum, couldn't think what woke her. She looked up at the ceiling and then at the door. Something made her get out of bed and go to the door. She could see someone on the step. It wasn't, was it? It was Angel.

Suha sat on the step next to her and put her arm around her. She felt Angel's body stiff against her. And as she held her, she began to relax.

"What is it, darling? Can't you sleep?, she asked Angel.

With that the dam burst - Angel wrapped her arms around Suha's waist tightly and began to cry in great shuddering sobs.

Suha was stunned. What could have happened to distress her to this extent - Angel was a child of the rainbow- bright as the sunshine, and riding on the wind, a true happy bunny. She was always shaking off the little grey bits that tried to stick to her, the little troubles of that point in life, and off she went, playing and being the bright little sunny Pollyanna that she had been since birth!

Unlike Henry, nothing seemed to upset her for long, not even getting hurt, nothing fazed her and nothing really made her fearful either- or so Suha thought until now, that is….

What on earth was bothering her? Suha tried to think over the day, the week, the fortnight and even the month to see quickly, to see if there had been something that Angel had been upset about.

Yes, Angel just kept reaching for the extra bits of chocolate and ice cream when she thought no one was looking. It was very difficult to wake her up in the mornings for school- she literally had to be carried out of bed most days and brushed, bathed, combed and dressed for school.

She seemed reluctant to go- she would hold on to Mum's hand for that extra moment and it was just her being a bit sticky, Suha thought. She would stand and wait for her to go through the school doors before she turned away, just to reassure her. She didn't really think much of it at all.

Funnily enough, now that she thought of it, she didn't seem to fight or to argue with her brother in the past days. She was quite quick to 'defend her toys and territory' normally. Nor chat like before, about the day or what she was thinking, which was pretty much all the time. Many times Suha felt the sound was still switched on, so she could hear Angel speak, but her mind had run out of material long ago. It always made Suha laugh out loud! She could really go on talking forever.

For that matter, neither did Henry say very much of late. Why didn't she pick it up before?

And then Angel began to speak in stops and starts at first and then in big rushes- school was not the same. There were these boys in her class who fought with each other and because she was friends with James, and not Crispin, Crispin would get into a fight with her and push her to the ground and hold her there! Sometimes they held her so tightly to the ground she couldn't breathe properly.

There were the other two boys too, Arnold and Hector who would be on Crispin's side and against Angel.

What was her mistake? Just that she was friends with James.

And they did that to her brother Henry too. Though he usually ran away and got less hurt than her.

"I can't run away, Mama," she said. "They are too strong for me and hold me to the ground- I can't breathe. Look at these bruises on my body."

As she spoke, Suha was stricken with sinking feeling of foreboding, a warning of the coming storm and an icy fear came over her. She felt an instant sweeping wave of protectiveness. She wanted to wrap Angel in her arms tightly and keep her close and safe from those rude and simply horrible and absolutely disgustingly obnoxious boys.

Then after a long time of sitting together and letting Angel cry it out, when she seemed calmer, Suha told her what she would do- "I'll come with you into school, darling," she said to Angel, "and I will go and speak to Mr Hammond, your Principal. He has always said no bullying is allowed in school so he will do something. I am sure he will."

Angel rested against Suha and seemed to absorb her calm and her energy and slowly she went to her room, to sleep. Her Mum was right perhaps. The principal did seem like a nice jolly man and he was quite strict about not running on the stairs, she remembered. This was so much worse than that. Last year, when Crispin drew on Henry's book, the teacher did call Mum in and explain to her. He said Crispin was upset that Henry had done so much better in the test and that why he had done this. He was punished for that. It would be alright.

Downstairs, Suha was in complete turmoil, raging inside- who do these children think they are and why were they coming to school and behaving like hooligans, bullying a classmate who had done them no harm at all!! And a classmate like Angel? Seemed totally ridiculous and not making any sense. And where were their wonderful parents? This is what they taught their children? Were their parents even aware of this? It seemed way unbelievably mean and dirty.

In the morning, Suha asked Henry about this and he said, "Yes, there are many instances when these boys have behaved really badly."

They went into school together. Suha, herself was not the kind to complain about a bit of roughness at play or a push or a shove on the playground, done by accident, either. But she had a very high sense of protectiveness towards these children of hers, who were, at the end of the day, only little and really not too able to seriously defend themselves against any organised or sustained attack like this.

Suha approached Mr Hammond hesitantly even then. She and her husband had moved to the country only a few years ago and since they had not been educated in England, though she had studied in France, she was apprehensive as she felt she did not know how these things were dealt with in practice, over here.

Smart looking Mr Hammond was a bit of a showman kind of person. He prided himself on what he called his family home-from-home kind of school set up. It was the gentlest way for children to learn to be away from home, at school and learning from some very experienced teachers. He took great pride in the fact that some of his staff had been there for a few decades. That was the strength of the school. Being one of the best pre-prep schools in town, they sent students each year to almost every school that was highly ranked in the league table of academically good schools in the city.

"Mr Hammond, can I ask you what your position on bullying is," she asked him, hesitantly.

Suha herself was one of the gentlest persons in the world. Everyone who knew her found her immensely capable and accomplished and also kind, helpful and full of fun and a fabulous sense of humour. Most often the complaint anyone could have about her was that she was "too nice"!!

"Oh, we have zero tolerance," he said. "Tell me what has happened," he said.

She told him all that Angel and Henry had told her.

"Leave it with me," he said.

In the afternoon, at pick up, he came over to Suha and said, "You know, Angel and Henry must be mistaken. There is no bullying of any kind going on. I was watching them at playtime and they are all playing happily together. They must have dreamed up the whole thing. We have such a happy school here and all the children are such good friends with each other. Let's just forget the whole thing shall we?"

Suha couldn't believe what she was hearing. Really? Were Angel and Henry making this up? And what about those bruises on her body?

Somehow she found her voice and said, "No, Mr Hammond. She has bruises on her body and she isn't one to complain- you know that too? She has not been sleeping well for the last two weeks already."

He seemed to think about what she said. "Well, I am happy to tell the other teachers to keep an eye out. Let us see for a few days if you insist," he said.

"Yes, I do insist, please," she said.

Okay, Suha thought. Hopefully it will be picked up by the teachers. After all, the children say it happens every day in class and at playtime.

Still hopeful, the three went home. "Try to tell me everything that happens at school everyday from now on," Suha said to the two of them.

And slowly they began to tell her all the really sad, horrible and mean things that been happening to them. Suha could see the two of them were so disturbed that they didn't want to go to the school any more.

"Why didn't you tell me before?," she kept asking them. "Please do tell me anything like this happening to you as soon as it happens. On the very same day, please. Every day I ask you how school was, and everyday you say, it was good. This is good? Is this even okay? This is really really bad, isn't it? It is making you unhappy, so why didn't you tell me about it straightway? I must know so I can try and sort it out with the school or help you or think of what to do about it. I am your mother," she kept saying, crying. What were they thinking, these two? And going through so many harrowing days at school. They must be so unhappy. And she thought they were just on the edge for some minor reason!

What can we do, she was thinking. It is year 2 and next term they have the 7+ assessments which decide which preparatory school they will go to. Both of them didn't want to go to mixed schools any more. This bullying explains it, she thought. She had wondered why they were so vehemently against mixed schools.

The next day, Suha tried to speak to their class teacher, Ms Williamson about it. Her response was totally different. "These two, Angel and Henry, are so bright, Suha," she said, "most of the other children are jealous of them. There will always be someone who tries to hurt them like this. I have no doubt they are being bullied, but there isn't anything I can do. I do try my best to tell those boys off, but as you can see, it has not done anything to change their behaviour at all. And this is the last year anyway. Everyone will hopefully be at different schools at the end of this."

Suha was so surprised she didn't know what to say. "What shall I do?, "she asked.

"Tell them to just go about their work quietly, and not say anything to anyone," she said. "Are you planning to speak to their parents?"

"I would like to, but if you are able to speak to them, I won't," Suha said.

"Okay, I'll speak to them," said Ms Williamson.

Another week passed. Angel was not sleeping well and neither she nor Henry were happy to go to school still.

Ms Williamson sent a handwritten note saying the same thing. The children are wonderful and Oh! So kind, gentle and amazing. They will have people jealous of them and trying to hurt them repeatedly, so it will be good for them to learn to be thick-skinned. She now changed her mind and wrote that she wasn't going to speak to any of the parents about this. And she was most insistent that Suha did not approach the parents either. If Suha did, she wrote, the school would deny any knowledge of the bullying and then Suha would be on her own. It sounded distinctly like a warning shot. She was being threatened now to drop the matter? At this crucial time when the tests were so close and to be done to their best effort? What best effort can children so disturbed put out?

And Really?? Six years old and they need to be okay with being pushed around and hit and held to the ground against their will, in a "Boy's Fight" for territory?

Are these animals warring for territory or children in pre-preparatory school?

It was now a good five weeks since Angel had slept well and she had dark circles around her eyes.They had no one to turn to, to even speak to, or ask for help or confide in leave alone seek redressal.

The assessments were coming up and things were not improving at all. The teachers and Mr Hammond seemed to have decided the matter was non existent.

Suddenly, things changed about their work too. All this time, Ms Williamson was so sure and had been writing notes to Suha about which schools, and they were ones with high emphasis on academics, they could be certain of gaining places for the two of them. Now, for some unknown reason, they seemed "not ready" and so would have to go to the nearby mixed school.

"What? You cannot be serious!!" Suha said to Ms Williamson.

Suha sat down with Henry and Angel and told them to leave all the negative stuff to one side and focus on the tests and only on the tests. After all, they needed to get places in their chosen preparatory schools too, right?

They agreed and the Christmas break went in practice tests and all the preparation they needed.

There was no let up on the bullying side of things, both from the teachers and the children now. The bullying didn't stop and the tests came and went. To their credit,

Angel and Henry did their tests to the best of their abilities. Suha was so proud of them.

The tests were done in the first week of January and then the results and calls for second rounds started coming in. They still had no one to speak to, or ask for help, or confide in, or seek guidance, or encouragement even.

To their credit, Angel and Henry did their tests to the best of their abilities and they felt good they had worked well.

There were interview calls for both so it was positive news and and slow upbeat feeling began to spread between them. Cautiously, they went about the interviews and to their delight every school they went to, the staff seemed to love both of them. In the short time they were at those schools for the interviews, the staff knew them by name and exchanged hearty chats with them, joked about and spoke to Suha too, about how lovely the children were. Things were going to be alright it seemed.

Then there came the message from one of the schools that we are sorry we cannot give a place to a child like

Henry. Suha and Sri took an appointment with the school and went over immediately to meet the Head.

Before they went, Suha, inspite of everything, went to the school to speak to Mr Hammond. She, very politely requested him to speak to the Head as well, from his side, and explain to him what a wonderful boy Henry is. He assured her he would. Suha believed him.

The Head of the new school met them with great enthusiasm and told them Henry had been very weak English, but had topped the Maths test- one of only two boys out of 208 to do so. His head of academics would never want to let such a boy go to any other school. That's why he did not mention it to the head of academics, that he was meeting the boy's parents! Sounded so strange. On the one had he was so enthusiastic about Henry and on the other, he was most insistent he wouldn't be able to give him a place.

But he was stuck on that they still could not take him on this year- "You put him in any school," he said, "doesn't matter which one. I will pick him up next year."

And why not this year? He simply refused to say why.

Suha and Sri came out of the meeting totally shaken and unable to understand this view and why the Head of the school was not able to give Henry a place.

Then came a letter for Angel, and along the same lines. They both went to meet the Head of that school. The lady Head was very kind and spoke with great concern. She said there is no way she could take Angel as the school report from her pre-prep school was not good at all, and so she cannot explain giving a place to a child whose report is so bad.

And the general view, she added, was that since it was a pre-prep school Angel went to, that ended at year 2, all children need to move on to other schools, so there seemed no good reason for the teachers to give Angel a bad school report. Except that there was a problem with the child!!

It was like having a ton of bricks fall on them. Suha and Sri had no words at all. They were so horrified, shocked, upset and in serious distress.

And it was as if they were mute spectators to the nightmare that played out in front of them and new nuances and new lows unfolding every day.

Suha went back to Ms Williamson and asked whether she had given a bad report. "Yes, I did as I did not think they could go to any school except this mixed school which has offered them a place". "But that's not the right one for them, you said so yourself," Suha still tried to reason with her. But Ms Williamson was adamant and closed to any further discussion. Suha then went Mr Hammond. Asked him why the school had given a bad report to these children who, no one, including he himself could deny, were so bright, any school would love to have them there.

His résponse shook Suha to the core. She could not believe, Mr Hammond could do this sort of lowdown act. This punching hard below the belt.

He said, "We didn't write a good report for them to go to any of those schools, because we would have to tell them that they may have seemed a little weak, if at all, in their assessments, because they have faced serious bullying. That would be serious for us. We would be admitting bullying took place at our school and it was serious enough to cause children as clever as these two, to do their assessments not very well.

Well, as I said before, we never saw it happen, so we cannot tell anyone it has happened. So as far as we are concerned, there was no bullying happening in our school."

What could she say to that?

She just came home and cried her heart out- loud sobs broke from deep within her it felt the earth would crack open and the skies would break down too! She felt so anguished that she had not only not been able to protect her little six year olds from such persistent and painful bullying, for absolutely no fault of theirs. She had also not been able to see that the school would royally breach trust and all the codes of education and propriety and mess up their education?? Could they really get away with this total injustice? Seems like they could. Who would take the word of a parent against that of the school?

What was left? What could she do? There was no other school test left and absolutely nothing they could do to change anything.

The conversation with the Head of the new boys school seemed to make complete sense now- it was the school report that had said the child was not suitable.

Who does this sort of thing in this day and age? Was there no recourse? Parents whose children are bullied had to go through the agony many times over, and they are not treated with all the due concern in such a delicate matter. That of six year old children.

Suha's mind was whirling with so many waves, all of rage and all coming to crash in her mind repeatedly. The voices in her head that screamed that this was all so wrong, were very loud and very clear. Her strong sense of justice shouted at her that this was a complete wrong and one that went against all that she had learnt, seen, heard and felt in her life, in all the many countries she had lived and in all the numerous cities, towns and villages that she had travelled to. Why, she herself had taken so steps to prevent abuse of any kind at her workplace and to safeguard all the people that came to work there, whatever their role. This was so wrong and it went against every fibre of her being. She was trying to stand and fight something she had no access to. As a parent, she was a complete outsider, she was a nobody in the school's eyes, and vulnerable since she had no way of fighting back, even of persuading the school with gentle words, as she had tried so hard to do.

Yes, Henry and Angel need to be strong and be able to push the bullies away, physically and mentally, and step away from any tough situation, but they were only six and at that age, should they not be protected, if they clearly could not do it themselves?

So, we need children to go to school ready to fight bullies in the form of children and in the form of teachers? That is the great example of education system, in this country, that has a global reputation for its education system being one of the best and among the most sought after in the world?

Was this why they moved here? To have the children and was this why they had chosen this pre-preparatory school, that was a few minutes walk from home. The warm family kind of nurturing atmosphere and superb pastoral care was supposed to be the highlight of the school.

This is what they have done to two bright six year olds? Suha asked herself again and again and with no answers.

What could they do now?

Suha sat Henry and Angel down and told them what all had happened- they asked why the school and the principal and the teachers were being so nasty. Suha explained it all happened because they had complained about the bullying. The school possibly felt they were not going to do that well in the tests and therefore wrote bad reports for them, so as not to let it affect the reputation of the school- imagine if they had given good and nice reports and Henry and Angel had done not so well in their assessments. The school would look bad, as if recommending children who were not so academically inclined.

The whole thing fell flat when these two did amazingly in the tests and got themselves the interview calls. To retrieve the situation and the reputation of the school, they continued to say there was never any bullying that happened there.

Suha and Sri took all their love and affection for Henry and Angel, spread it and wrapped them tenderly in it, like a warm safe blanket, so they felt warm, cocooned and most of all loved. To the high heavens and back. To precious bits.To the depths of the oceans too.

"It is something really bad that has happened but that doesn't mean you are bad at all. In fact, you are so good, we think you should just be quiet about it and go to school and do your work as usual," Suha said to them.

"In a few more weeks it will be holidays and then you only have one short summer term before you never go back to this school again."

Both Angel and Henry said they didn't want to go to this school at all because their classmates were being horrible and Ms Williamson and her assistant were very discouraging too. They criticised their work all the time and made really hurtful remarks about it. One time she asked them to put their work into the bin straight after they did it as she couldn't even bring herself to look at it- it was of such a poor standard!!

Wouldn't a mother's heart feel like someone was plunging a knife into it and wriggling it around at will, to cause ever increasing pain? To listen to this sort of treatment of little six year old children, at school, of all places in the world.

But Suha had to be strong and calm, for the little ones' sake.

She said, "I cannot do anything else for you, I am sorry. But let's make a chart and set out how many more days we need to go to this school. Let us cross off the days as we go along.

And let us not think about this school or anything to do with it at all.

Pretend you are in a bubble. It is just you there. You two can play with each other or not at all. You can say you don't want to play and go and read a book if you want. You don't need to speak to anyone or go to anyone's home for a playdate or have anyone over, since they are all being so horrible. And I will be there at the door when the school ends, and we will come home together and do loads of lovely fun things together. We will go away for the holidays and go see movies or drive to the countryside during the weekends too.

How does that sound?"

The little darlings agreed.

Every day Suha dropped them to school and every afternoon she was there to collect them before time- she could never be late. She took treats for them every single day and they talked about where they would go next or what they would do.

But every single day she would end up crying like her heart was breaking inside her, at this injustice and the absolute ease with which it happened. With such a casual attitude, Mr Hammond and Ms Williamson had gone about wrecking havoc into the lives of the little children, Angel and Henry. All because she complained about their bullying!

Each day her heart was literally in her mouth, wondering how the children were going through the day, and every afternoon she would marvel at their maturity and their absolute mind-blowing calm. They never fussed to go to school and never came out crying or looking sad- but the moment they were in the car and driving off, she could see them visibly relax. Their shoulders would loosen and they would first check the snack bag out and once they were munching away on a favourite snack, they would begin to talk about what to have for dinner.

What could she possibly have done to have such wonderful little ones, who were going through something that would have broken an adult! She was thanking her stars, ancestors, Gods and Goddesses and every one she could possibly think of, with a full heart.

Each day, Angel and Henry would meticulously cross out the day that was gone, bringing them ever closer to never having to go to that school again.

What shocked Suha and simply beggared belief was Ms Williamson calling her in for a meeting during the term. She was positively gushing, telling her how wonderful Henry and Angel were at their work. "These children are simply the best anyone can wish for. See how amazing their work is," she said. Her assistant was as gushing too. They seemed to have only the highest positive adjectives to describe the children and more importantly, their work.

Suha simply thanked her and left. She couldn't think of a single thing to say, nor a single thing that would negate all that had happened, rather, all that had been wilfully done by the school. To be fair, she couldn't trust herself to be polite either.

Angel was sensitive to her mother's continuing distress and told her, "Mum, Henry and I were reading this story I had written some time ago. Do you remember it? We have so much to be thankful for. We can win and be positive. Nothing can hurt us again!"

They sat on the step and read it together again.

The story went…..

I am Green Pea, an alien from planet Zorgo. Our planet is split into different sections; green [food], blue [water], orange [houses] and the last one is red [warmth]. But we had a problem- the food was fading. We need help and fast.

Me and a few fellow friends swooped down to plant Blugren and saw an unforgettable sight- never would we forget it! Weird monsters holding strange objects.

"Mind reading," said Green Bean, my brother. Strange, very strange indeed. We grabbed a monster and flew back to Zorgo. We put a strange device on the monster's head and spoke Zorgish, but it translated to 'We need your help, our food is fading. Help.'

We grabbed food from Blugren and planted it, but we need another solution for the food just kept fading. We were impatient and asked it to tell us fast, 'what else' - the monster only answered weakly 'positive'. We asked again.

This time the monster answered softly 'energy'. I was utterly confused 'What on Zorgo, I thought!'

Green Bean said 'Positive energy! Of Course!'

We had the answer but not the monster. Rise from the ashes fall to the ashes. We spread the news as we pointed the gun to the houses and spread secret messages, thick and fast, of happy thoughts. Happy, happy thoughts!

For breakfast we used to ration the food- but we didn't to need anymore, as the food grew back and quickly too.

We had made the mistake. We had forgotten what our ancestors told us -

'Be thankful for what we have'. Always.

Positive Energy saves the day! The End!

Angel took Suha by the hand and said, "Mum, let's go and make a fresh start. Positive energy will bring us to our goal."

The three of them walked out of the school for the last time with their heads high and full of pride at having faced all the gross injustices thrown in their way, with such grace, dignity, maturity and resilience!

Of course, we will win, Mum! That was enough for Suha! These little ones had found their way!! And what was more, they were showing her the way too.

Kanyadaan- The "giving" of the daughters in marriage

Mili hawain me udenki yeh sazaa yaaron, ke main zameen ke rishton se kat gaya yaaron

Wo bekhayal musafir main raasta yaaron, kahan tha basme mere usko rokna yaaron!

The price of soaring high into the skies is that I have been cut off from my ties here on earth,

He was an unthinking traveller and I was the way, how could I make any move to stop him?

Akshara parked her car and walked into the office. It was with the same feeling as every day. She felt she was entering a cocoon, a world so different from her own. A world where every man and woman seemed to outdo each other to be more conservative, or come across as more restrictive in their list of "can be done" or "cannot be done" by girls- never mind, that these girls were highly qualified professionals. They could take anyone on, in their chosen field and take a master class for the others, in how things should be done !!!

Every work day she stepped into this bubble and throughout the day she listened and made herself not react at all, to the contrary, act as if this was all normal and how it should be, to any of the target practice sort of jibes, generously sent her way by her fellow workers.

Another one was the cosseting or overprotective attitude the men showed the women in the company. As if they needed to be covered up in cotton wool and spirited away to the interior of the company lest some proverbial wicked wolf was lurking nearby. Even the security chief was into this game. Ever since the day he saw her chatting with the managing director, he made sure she was properly escorted to the office floor. What he did not know was that, meeting the managing director and the board of directors, apart from the senior persons in the company, was part of her everyday job as a senior manager in the investment bank, reporting directly to the managing director.

She smiled and took his fussing over her without a murmur. He would even toss other "lesser mortals" out of the lift without hesitation. Every morning she arrived thinking how she could try and bypass his attention without seeming rude. With no success yet.

She sat down at her desk and wondered for the millionth time what on earth she was thinking when she took this job in the company that was so traditional in its approach- sorry, she thought, she needed to rephrase that.

No, it was not the fault of the company. It was these conservative minds she worked with. At least one "candidate", as she called her enlightened colleagues, came forward, every single day, to ask if her parents could not afford to keep her at home, or, could her parents not be marrying her off soon?? Or, on variation days, were her parents actually okay with living off her earnings? Did they not feel upset that they lived in a home which had a girl bring in a salary?

They had no clue what her background was, or who her parents were. Come to think of it, they did, in a manner of speaking. They had no doubt she belonged to the highest caste there was, the Vaidiki Velanadu Brahmins, the absolute possible top of the top, in the caste food chain. She still shook her head at the thought, that people could be hired not for their looks or abilities, even that seemed so unreal to her, but for their caste! Their accident of birth determined their employability. No one in the company was a "non brahmin" as they put it, with so much condescension.

Thinking of the atmosphere back at her home, and then making the inevitable comparison with the one at work, the work one was so incongruous, so out of sync, she couldn't help smiling. Smiling at her inability to comprehend it. Smiling at her helplessness to change it, in any way.

Where could one even begin to explain that one needs to respect all individuals not because of where they were born but because of who they are and what they have made themselves into.

She remembered visiting the home of Benjamin Disraeli, three time Chancellor of Britain, and a very learned and capable man. Born a Jew, he educated himself and became a leading personality of his time. This was the way a common man could aspire to greatness, as without the 'good fortune" of being born into nobility, and that meant sure acceptance into society, there was no route to such acceptance. Becoming a member of parliament was forbidden to non christians so he converted to Christianity and then became a member of the British parliament. Laws were, of course, changed later to allow people of all faiths to become members of parliament. But even a person as capable as Disraeli had to fix his religious attachments before he could aspire to public office.

It was true the power was in the hands of the learned everywhere and since some were inclined to learning more, they were taught. Soon enough the groupings began and those that were taught were not doing anything else and those that weren't, were not taught at all. Great kings went through their lives without the advantage of literacy, relying solely on their religious scholars to interpret any texts, or to do all the writing or reading for them.

But that was ancient times, and these were supposedly the very modern and progressive times. And yet, the world around her seemed to be in this time warp. Nothing had changed from long long ago.

What could be the obsession of people to worship

and prostrate themselves, with a almost hysterical frenzy before the Goddess, looking upon Her as the Mother, the Savior, the giver of Strength, the Rescuer of last resort in cases where even the Gods had failed to do so, and yet, almost without skipping a beat, mourn the birth of a daughter!

Her birth is marked with a period of glumness and kind of 'at least the mother and child are safe' kind of 'feeling of last resort. Not only were the sweets, if any were even distributed at her birth, downgraded from the mighty laddoo, to a minor barfi, the whole idea of the child's future was even in question. No expense really needed to be dipped into and indulged to educate or bring her up as they would perhaps a male child, but the collective drooping of the parents and in many cases, the families shoulders, with the burden of the presence of the girl child, that needed, now to be endured by all of them, was palpable from Day One, for sure.

There was no time to rejoice. Everyone visiting the newborn would come, check the baby out and if she checked the boxes of being fair skinned, lovely eyed and so on, sort of pat the parents on the shoulder or back as if to say, at least she's decent looking so you may not have a problem when the time comes, to unburden this load.

Problem with what? Marrying her off, of course! And that was the target event that would reduce the burden on these poor parents shoulders. God was taking their test, it seems.

There are families today, who don't distinguish between male and female offspring and educate and bring up the children in a similar way. These 'progressive' folk too, seem to suddenly take a time machine leap into the past century, or so, when this girl child comes to a 'marriageable age'.

They joined the ranks of the rest of the folk who were waiting to shed their burdens as soon as an opportunity in the form of a 'decent proposal' presented itself. Nothing the girl said or did could make them change their minds.

Not only that, such a girl, highly educated, qualified and at the cutting edge of her profession, well placed and fully capable in every way, including being financial independent, was given lessons in the form of continuous drip lectures, on how she should be subservient, gentle, kind, loving, serving and never speaking her mind, in her marital home, especially not to her in laws or her husband even.

Akshara remembered reading the story of the great Sultan of the Ottoman Empire, Suleiman, the Magnificent. He had a son from his first wife and his second and favourite wife gave birth to four sons and one daughter. Though they loved her dearly, the girl, Mihrimah, knew her mother mourned her birth. Giving birth to sons alone made the woman strong in the harem and also strong in the eyes of the people as well as the Sultan himself. Mihrimah knew this and did not hold it against her mother. Her parents brought her up very lovingly and her wishes were truly commands for the palace staff. Her mother had a very close relation ship with her and taught her all the intricacies and subtle nuances of court and harem politics.

And yet, when she grew to a marriageable age, her parents arranged hers with a governor of one of the Empire's provinces. Her mother, who had encouraged

her to fall in love, just as she and her father had, explained
to her that she had to agree to the marriage, as it would
secure her brothers, who were princes in their own right's,
future. In one single stroke all the ideas and thoughts she
had of her own future and how she would write it, were
destroyed. Never to be visited again. And she, Mihrimah,
died before she had ever lived. No, she did get married and
have children and all the rest of it, but the spark that was
her, had left her on her wedding day.

And her thoughts were of herself when she went
through, in her eyes, the funereal wedding. She had been
mourned by everyone including her mother, the day she
was born, and yet, she and she alone could rescue them
all from a terrible fate that would come their way, if she
did not make this marriage. Where was the morality or
any basic sense of decent human values here? Mihrimah
herself couldn't condone their expecting her to give up her
whole life, basically, entering into an arrangement called
marriage, like this, but she went through it nevertheless,
and without complaint or any hatred directed towards
either her mother, for suggesting it, or her brothers for

not being even able to protect themselves, leave alone protect her.

This, of course was in 1540. If one did not know the date, one may clearly be excused for thinking this is the modern day story.

Nothing had changed, indeed.

When she was a child, Akshara's grandfather, a very learned Vedic scholar, would speak to her at length about the vedas, the religious books in Hinduism dating back thousands of years. They have, written in them the essence of life and how one can have a good life, what one must practice, and so on. Everything, in fact.

'Do you know what is the biggest Danam, the biggest act of charity in the world, according to the Vedas? It is the Kanyadanam! The gift of the girl child in marriage, the ritual of giving away of the daughter. That is also the custom in many parts of the world. The girl, the bride, is always given in marriage to the man, the groom.

One of the purposes of life is to free oneself of the debts that one accumulates over one's lifetime and this process of accumulation begins at birth.

The highest debt one is ever under, is that of the Mother that gives birth!! As she, like the Earth, provides the fertile ground for the child, to grow and prosper. The next, is the father, like the giant Sky above us. Perhaps dual income families are more de rigeur now, but earlier it was only the man earning, to allow his family to live, grow and equip themselves for their futures.

The best friend one can ever hope to have in life, is the spouse, husband or wife, and the best sort of friendship, where one can, more importantly share every single one of one's thoughts, and the partner becomes the repository of one's concerns. When one is fully understanding of the other's failings rather than strengths alone- that is when the spouses have a true and deep relationship.

And a non judgmental and open one. To be seen, heard or experienced just like their own selves. In full measure. The talk she heard recently came to mind. So simply put.

Relationships can become full of harmony when we practice the including of another soul in our life, and not management of the thoughts of another soul. Every colour that the relationship has, can be experienced and cherished in its own way. In this kind of interlacing between two souls, differences in opinion don't seem to cause any alarm. By embracing simplicity and enhancing our own way of being, bead by bead, stitch by stitch, new and beautiful relationships are woven naturally on their own.

And most importantly, a relationship is not always about thinking about someone. Feelings of love, care and respect are about our own self too. When connections are routed in soul consciousness, it is no more about give and take. If we are able to identify our originality as pure souls, relationships become more and more visible as an exchange of energy. We understand that it is just one of the aspects of our lives, and that we don't have to structure our lives around it. So much of our potential would then find expression in various ways that we have not imagined.

Expectations are like rocks in your path, they just trip you up.

Was this last bit the truth about the relationship? She should have no expectations? But were it not for expecting a relationship to start, build and last, why would she even contemplate something like a marriage?

Why put so much effort into getting to know anyone and his whole family, meeting their sometimes never ending and very insistent and persistent expectations, simply to achieve soul consciousness and feel it was all like the old adage,"neki car darya me daal" or do the good deeds and throw that into the sea, meaning, have no expectation of, or even an acknowledgement for the deeds.

But that is a good deed, not a life being lived with someone.

The path to soul conciousness was through living this life and not by renouncing it. That much she understood.

Akshara's Grandfather, the Vedic scholar, had explained to her that the highest form of "Daanam" or giving in charity, is Kanyadaan, the giving of the bride in marriage to the groom and in many cultures, also to the whole family. No one ever gave away a groom!

His explanation was that to achieve salvation the surest way, was to give your daughter in marriage, so really, heaven help the parents who had no daughters!

The daughter is considered the highest form of gift to give away in an act of charity, as the parents take care of her, nurture her and educate her in the formal form of education, to read and write and all the rest of it, but also in how to run household. They make sure she knows how to make purchases and manage finances for the household, how to cook all the varieties of food and serve them too. She is taught the importance of being patient in matters that are important and when the other person is flustered or impatient. How to advise when it is sought for, how to be silent when the situation demands it.

Karyeshu Dasi, Karaneshu Manthri, Bhojeshu Mata, Shayaneshu Rambha, Roopeshu lakshmi, Kshamayeshu Dharitri,

Satkarma Nari, Kuladharma Patni.

The Dharmapuranas, the Sacred Texts, say an ideal wife, is one, who does good deeds, is one who works like a servant, advises like a minister, feeds like a mother, makes love like a nymph, is as beautiful as Goddess Lakshmi, and forgiving like the Mother Earth.

And the parents give such a fully accomplished

daughter in marriage to the groom. Any guesses how one should take care of such a priceless gift?

There is also given, the guidance for caring and teaching a boy too, so he may grow into a man worthy of receiving such an amazing gift.

Karyeshu Yogi, Karaneshu Daksha, Rupecha Krishna,

Kshamayathu Rama, Bojyeshu Truptha, Sukhadukkha Mitra,

Shatkarmayuktha, Khalu Darmanatha.

Work without expecting any result; have patience, and caliber to maintain his family;

Be like Lord Krishna, always smiling and happy; And be patient and forgiving like Lord Rama and follow all the orders of the Father;

Never criticise the food served by the wife or the mother: and be a friend in happiness and in sorrow.

It would be laughable if it wasn't so utterly deplorable, that most people are not even aware of the existence of this guidance. It remains, of course, to be seen, if it makes an iota of a difference, if they knew it existed. Would most people care to teach their sons to be worthy husbands if they married. Like the stand up comedian put it, the most parents expect from their sons is that he is born and that's it. If he listens to one or two things they say, that is a bonus feature.

Where does one go from here, Akshara thought. Her interest in the structure of relationships and the balance between sexes was driven by her new thought process. She was really trying to see if all this progressiveness was just skin deep, or could be applied positively to her boyfriend, Sean.

Was he safe, meaning, in her eyes, did he check these boxes of being respectfully equal to her or was he paying mere lip service. That was her task, to unravel the real Sean.

In the world around her, a man's stubbornness is taken to be his self respect and a woman's self respect is taken to be her stubbornness. Women are taught to forgive the biggest mistakes of their husbands, while committing none of their own and if they ever did, being ready for the punishment that they were now deserved, to be complied in full measure.

If the husband ever was in the agony of physical

pain, the interpretation of the feeling would be that he is immersed in guilt and showing remorse. Really?

Akshara thought of Sean, her boyfriend. That was the only way to describe him. Looks wise, he was attractive with a lopsided smile and a huge mop of hair that kind of begged someone to dig their fingers in and rake it up. He wore only three colours, black, grey and white. He spoke in a deep voice and loved to pull jokes on her, with a completely straight face. He claimed he followed the path of least resistance, meaning he said yes to most suggestions, all without every having the slightest intention of going over or doing whatever it was he was agreeing with at the time, In fact, he never seemed bothered to remember what he had agreed to, to the frustration of people around him. He was, however, very popular, and most felt kind of honoured when he chose to interact with them. He seemed very gentle and kind of doglike in his hanging around her sometimes.

He was her colleague at work and they had worked closely on many transactions. It was perhaps a side effect, or, an effect nevertheless, of their working together, that they became more comfortable with each other. They typically spent long hours doing, either the number crunching, that was a primary part of figuring out whether the deal made sense to first take up, and then, to do on their own as a bank, or to bring in other banks as a consortium, or, on other days, to make the intricate and highly personalised presentations that were part of the sales act, either to companies or to the buyers, whether institutions or individuals.

This was the primary nature of their work. Helping companies raise money via debt or equity, meaning through borrowing or share issues. The work also meant she travelled to where the clients were and sometimes around the world, for the pre capital raising marketing.

Sometime the travel was short trips but sometimes it dragged over weeks and it was on these trips that she became friends with Sean.

He too, came from and similar family background and was educated in similar institutions like herself, degrees in corporate law, financial management and a masters in business management. He too, wore his abilities lightly, not quick with sarcastic retorts or massive put downs, that were commonly passed off in the banks, as the behavioural done thing parlance. She had lost track of the number of times her colleagues suggested overtly or covertly, all without turning a hair, that she should perhaps sleep with the client to seal the deal. That was among the milder ones.

He was quick with numbers as well and they both were very hard workers. They both aspired to perfection. They were keen to put in the extra bite into their presentations, that the clients seemed to appreciate, and so it could be safely said they were on a solid career path as far as their work life was going.

She began to play their interactions over in her mind and she was taken by surprise. There were differences which she had simply glossed over at the time. Perhaps she was just wanting to get the work finished, or perhaps she, being the kind of person she was, would almost never expect the person on the other side to behave in a manner less than that of her own. Including even when the said person had misbehaved earlier. For the god only knows kind of reason, that's how she was. Always had been.

When she thought of how they worked together, she remembered she was always in charge of arranging for coffee, or if it was mealtime, the meal for that time of day. Much as she thought about it, she couldn't find one instance where he had done that. And perhaps what was worse still, he encouraged others to pile their loads on to her, saying she can easily do it. He never tidied up after, either. Somehow it was her task to do that. It wasn't that she balked at any of the tasks she called ancillary, like these, but to be a designated housekeeper, merely because she was female, was a bit much, was it not? Come to think of it, it was a tiny task and easily accomplished too, especially when each did their own bits, as they saw done in their partner banks or abroad even. Was it an 'Indian' way of thinking lining the bottom of that brain of his?

The time she was in the meeting with the lawyers to set the time line for the public issues and finished late. When it finished she gathered up her papers only just realising how really late, in fact, it was. She hadn't time to call Sean even and tell him she was tied up. No! She remembered his parents were visiting and they were supposed to go out for a meal together. She was still whirring mentally with all the dates and deadlines she had to juggle for this, even for the small amount though, they were raising for that client. She came out of the room, and was hurrying to make the call to Sean, to tell him they should go ahead and she would join them later, when the security guard came up to her to say there was a car parked outside for her to drive home in perhaps, and it had her parents in it. He didn't know, of course, that they were Sean's parents and not hers.

Shocked, she made the call to Sean and he told her he was busy, so he had brought his parents over and left them in the car so she could take them to dinner and he would join later. 'I was in a meeting too, Sean,' she had said at the time. His response, 'You seem to be done now so just take them to dinner'. How was this even okay, she remembered thinking. Wasn't there something really missing here. How could he be so presumptuous to assume she would 'do the needful' and he need not have taken the responsibility, even when those visiting were his parents. He could just assume she would drop or wind up her work as soon as she was given this task and present herself to take charge of his parents. He had no compunctions at all about putting her perhaps, to any inconvenience, as a result of this. Or the embarrassment she felt and continually apologised to his parents for, throughout the evening, because they had to wait in the car outside her office, regardless of the fact that she had no knowledge of their waiting in that way, or that it wasn't her responsibility in the first place. She was surprised at his treating the whole thing as a matter of fact event, one that was meant to happen and in that way as well. What and where could she begin to explain what was wrong with the whole sequence of events, to someone who merely saw the entitlement to call on her, almost at will, one would hazard to presume.

The little instances seemed to add up, she realised. Over time there had been many of them and in multiple situations. Even the seemingly unromantic rejoinder when she asked, after they had seen a film together, whether he would stand and protect her, if she was ever attacked, like the woman in the film. His answer was that he wouldn't, because it would mean he needed to put himself in harm's way as well, and that he would not do. Even her persistent questioning or trying to laugh it off as unromantic that he was not wanting to help rescue his girlfriend, did not change his mind.

He just did not see it as sharing a bond or sharing responsibilities in any of these tasks.

It was becoming apparent that he had decided views on her appearance too. What she wore was an open ended subject, one that he could comment on, forcefully at times when she protested that she was not inappropriately dressed or on days she was really upset, that he had no say in the matter. That seemed to wind him up more and he became sulky and difficult to talk to. The whole outing was in jeopardy, if they were out, and if they were are work, he gave her weird looks all day. There were times she simply rushed to the shops nearby, since her home was far away from her workplace, to purchase a change of clothes. Duly mollified, he seemed happy to play boyfriend again.

It was sometimes such a quick incident. If she could call it that.

One so short that if Akshara blinked, she may have thought she was imagining the whole thing. Many a time, she had to shake herself out of the burst of hurt she felt and the righteous indignation at the injustice of it. Was it something she had misread or misheard or misinterpreted? Her heart was always on the back foot before ascribing any negative to anyone. That was just her. So she went on questioning the reality of something she should have accepted as true and happening to her, long before this, and taken the call on the facts, either way. She should have sought to protect herself from this subtle form of abuse, for there was no other way of describing it, rather than continue to expose herself to more.

Therein lay the dilemma for her. She was trying to invest in a relationship in an honest way, and according to her girl friends, this sort of accusations or tantrums were common enough in their relationships too. The true dilemma was ever deeper. There was no infidelity or drunken stupors or a gambling habit or even bad language being hurled at her, that she could say stop, 'this isn't what I am due. I deserve more respect than this and the freedom to be me. Not someone who you think you want as me.'

The covert form of abuse was hidden in such a beautiful velvet glove, if she had not been on the receiving end of it, she would certainly question the abuse was there.

Sometimes she did feel weary of it all, she realised. The tension of what might upset Sean was a little knot, that was always in there, in her mind. A fear she was needlessly living with. She was just looking for a little respect and a little affection, where she was showering loads of both.

Was that too hard to get, in a relationship, especially one that claimed to be the truest and most honest of friendships between two people. Were there no people in the modern world who gave and took in the same measure, the good in a meeting of mind and body, that was equal in all respects, each bringing their own complete and beautiful selves to make a twosome, that could ride the biggest of waves on the strongest of seas, safely and with all their mutual respect and love, like a much beloved and warm rug, safely around them?

These ups and downs seemed incongruous with Sean's public persona, or the face he showed, the manners he wore, whether at work or at social settings, when they were with other people. The chinks appeared only when they were alone. That made it harder for her to ask anyone's opinion on the subject, just to get another person's view on it, or just about talking about the issue, which may help him behave differently perhaps, or show him he was wronging her with his narrow thinking. She could hardly bring up incident out of the blue, bang in the middle of a conversation with friends or relatives. There was usually no possible context to put it in, and for some reason, he seemed to have built up such a reasonable image of a concerned and caring individual, of balanced and fully supportive views, no one, including his parents would entertain even a suggestion that it wasn't, in fact, so. That he was capable of being this difficult, traditional and forcefully conservative person was not something that came to anyone's mind really. Where would she begin, even if she wanted to?

Where, indeed, was she to go from here?

While her parents may be eagerly waiting to give away the 'apple of their eye' to achieve the ticket to the pathway to heaven, or salvation, or freedom from their parochial ancestral debts, she was initially hesitant to admit to herself but became slowly sure that, she was, in no way, ready to indulge their need. This was to be her 'Kanyadaan', and one with a price tag she wasn't prepared to pay. She owed that to herself.

The journey of the girl, whether Mihrimah from the 1540s or Akshara's personal one, from the 2021s, still had some way to go.

Magic. Again?

Apne haathon ki lakeeron me basa Le mujhko, Mai
hoon tera to Naseeb was apna banale mujhko-

Vaada phir vaada hai Mai zeher bhi pi jaun 'Qateel',
Shart yeh hai koi baahon me sambhale mujhko!

Let me be embedded like the lines your hands, make
me your destiny.

A promise is a promise and I am ready to drink poison
to keep mine, my only condition is that my beloved's arms
hold me tight!

Shruti ran to the door and opened it. There he stood.
Shekar, with his suitcase and his heart-skipping-a-few-
beats smile. Like something that stepped clean out of her
imagination. What on earth was he doing here anyway. A
thousand thoughts seemed to be pushing their way around
in a great mishmash.

Like the click of the shutter. Blink.

I have to tell you this, Shruti. It is what I've been
waiting for all this time. The offer has come through.

Which one is that?

The stint in Singapore. The global team is wanting me to join them.

Really? That is superb, Shekar. I think its time they recognised your abilities, no?

My abilities. Hmmmm. I think it is a brilliant opportunity to make the career leap.

I have to say, my dear Shekar, I told you so!

I know, Shruti. I was reluctant and feel comfortable here. I've been successful and getting up in the company, but when I was talking to the global team, I could see what the next level is really all about. My boss's boss may think the time has come for us to show the rest of the world how to run their business, but there is so much for us to learn as well.

Obviously, Shekar, my sweet, there is a catch, or I am missing the but?

No no no no no no no, Shruti. No catch at all. It is all good actually. They've offered a global role and will take care of my move, housing and living expenses. The way it is structured, I will have a bit of saving too. They want me to be there in six weeks. I thought we can take a bit of a break and holiday before the move.

Yes, of course. I know we've just bought the flat here, so we need some cash coming in to pay the loan for it. And if you think it is amazing, you should give it a good go. Move there.

What? Me? Move there? Alone? Aren't you going to move with me?

What will I do there, Shekar? And now? When I am in such a good position at my work. You have been building up to a good international break with all your seven day work schedule and constant travel all over the country. That it has come, is a great next step for you. Not now though for me...

Then when, Shruti? From what I have seen and talked with so many friends and colleagues, the financial services industry is totally booming and Singapore is well positioned and strongly emerging as the new finance centre. You will have great opportunities there. My darlingest Shruti, how can you even think I will go without you?

Shekar, I cannot think you will go anywhere without me too. Then again, you know my work. Also, at this time, I am in the middle of so many things here. I can't think of even taking a weekend off, really.

I can't believe you said that.

Said what, Shekar?

Just what you just did. Said you won't come with me, Shruti. To Singapore. Here I am thinking how we both will take a bit of a break- God and I know how much we need it, after the serious and continuous slogging we've been doing all of the past three years, here, in Mumbai.

But I seriously cannot take any break for a few weeks at least, Shekar. For sure.

I understand, Shruti. I want you to focus on your work and complete all your assignments. I am not saying walk out in between. That would be unprofessional and neither of us are okay with that. We can go for a break after that. Maybe drive around New Zealand? We've been planning to go there for a long while now, isn't it?

And that seemed to end the discussion for the time being.

Blink.

Shruti was in the present looking at the much loved face in front of her.

They took a step towards each other and then, absolutely in motion picture fashion, flew into each others arms. They held each other tight as if they were moulded into one, barely breathing, as if afraid it would shatter the moment, and yet aware of the other completely, with every single fibre of their being. They stood together for a while and then broke away to arms length.

There were so many questions Shruti had, but wait. No questions really. He was here and that's what mattered, didn't it?

She was content with her world around her again.

Shekar too, was so content just being in the moment. She was such a big part of his being, it was very difficult to be away from her for him as well.

For her, she could simply feel the knowledge of him seep into every pore of her being, like a million candles lit inside of her and spreading a warm and gentle glow all through her being.

Blink.

The seemingly endless evenings she had spent trying to think herself into a state of contentment with his thoughts and failing each time, falling into a retake of a restless sleep, resulting in a much tousled state of morning afters.

The Vipassana techniques came to mind. Where one withdrew into a silence that allowed one to focus on the inner self, the questions that filled the mind. The silence made the mind mull over the questions and with the result, the questions became the answers. Just like the mind, perhaps peeling away at the layers of the question, thereby clearing the fog in the mind, and what remained was the answer, clearly revealed. It was a much revered technique to the followers of Vipassana.

Shruti had tried this on herself again and again, to ask herself the question in silence, and keep asking the question, in the hope that the question will become the answer she was seeking.

Seeking it so desperately, it was like a flesh wound in her body, raw and hurting. She could not come to terms with his leaving at the end of their struggle to keep both going, their marriage and their careers, both of which were brilliant. And going really well at the time.

They had the jobs people would give their eye teeth for, and a marriage people would want to know the secret to, at any cost, as well. Both understood each other's hunger to do their work well, as well as to do well at their work. Their hunger to succeed at what they did, their professionalism, the meticulous conscientiousness, the natural curiosity and logical capability with which they tackled their jobs, her tough investment banking role and his head of national sales position.

They both shared a rapport where they could reach out to the other for a chat, help, advice and suggestions on their jobs, the people they worked with and their bosses too. Anything, as a matter of fact, and everything. They seemed to collect a posse of human behaviour manual kind of bosses too. They had such hilarious times somedays, talking about what happened earlier in the day.

It was a ritual with them. Both came out of work and on the way home, or, after they got back, changed and had their dinner, they would sit or lie close to each other, comfortably, and talk their day through. Sometimes it was more her and sometimes he had loads to talk about. Sometimes they both just had a seriously normal day so they had not much to talk about.

Even then, they sat together in a very comforting silence and then went to bed. Some days Shruti had to give the Americans a market update at about ten in the night and that was the last thing before bed.

At weekends, the timetable was sacrosanct. Saturdays, he still had half a days work, so she went shopping and got some errands done, picked up a few treats before lunch and once they had lunch they spent the whole afternoon playing games like scrabble, or going to meet friends.

It wasn't often they had people over for dinner. Usually they went over. When they did, Shekar was very particular to tell Shruti- 'Don't try to make fun of me.' To which she always laughed and said, 'learn to laugh at yourself.'

It wasn't as easy as all that. His classmates, when they met, would try to pull his leg, and if they did, Shruti, who had a very low threshold for humour, promptly burst out laughing. Which got him hopping mad. So the moment they left the friends' home, he would launch into, 'You have no sense, you don't care for what I tell you. I say I don't like it and you keep doing it.'

Shruti could never understand what made him so upset. She wasn't the one making the jokes, yes, she was laughing at them but it would seem rather rude to not laugh at the joke. What would the friends think. After all, they were mates from business school and above all, he too, was smiling at the joke. How could she possibly tell if he was smiling out of politeness, or because he was genuinely amused at what he was being poked with.

And so on it went. When they went to his bosses home, which was at fairly regular intervals too, since he, the boss, was really keen on 'building a close relationship' with Shekar and wanted his wife to build one with Shruti. Shruti, for her part, couldn't take much of these evenings at all. There was not much conversation as there were a bunch of subordinates and a boss, along with the boss's wife and the rest of the wives, who seemed like they were reluctant guests at a funeral. Hi, hello, how is work and how is life and then no one knew what to say.

Where the men were into a deep discussion, perhaps on the thirty fifth slide, of an intense power point presentation defending the sales figures, which were a twelve percent increase year on year, compared to a possible fourteen point three-five percent that it should have been, for the month, the women were desperately trying to look engaged, or for things to say, or even more desperately trying unsuccessfully to catch their husband's eye to say come over and help with this stagnating conversation.

Their drinks flowed like the quick brooks that skipped on the stones and hurried towards the next one, so also, they were in a hurry to bottoms up this drink and begin making inroads into the next one. Dinner would finally be served and the menu was repetitive as well. One could hardly blame the poor boss's wife, who had to make the effort to cook for and feed the lot of them who showed up regularly at her door.

The drive back home was always a churlish one. Shekar upset, as he had to go through this too much drink plied on him situation, as well as, a not-in-the-diary-but-yet-happening work meeting on a holiday, and Shruti, because she was not happy to spend her evening doing something she didn't want to do. Would he ever say he couldn't come to his boss's dinner? Not in her lifetime, it seemed. He just wished the boss would have a brainwave of reality striking and stop inviting them to these sort of dinners.

They would both curl up around each other as if to comfort the other, and go to sleep.

Visits to her boss's home or office parties were much in the same mould. Though, being "international' as opposed to an "Indian" company, they wouldn't talk shop, but there seemed to be a serious note of condescension in the bankers versus the other "non" professions of the world.

That got both of them seriously wound up by the end of the evening.

Sundays were precious. Sundays were lazy days. Spent getting up late, breakfast in bed, lots and lots of beautiful love making, and in so many times and ways that by the time they slept again, exhausted with all the lovemaking, and woke, it was late afternoon.

They would make so love so many times and with so much care and patience, that they both were riding on the climaxes they could reach for and grab with both hands. They were in ecstasy with each others bodies and were so eager to please each other. All the favourite spots were revisited. All the ice cream in the house, if there was any available, was put to good use to bring one peak after another of joyous, passionate and very comforting pleasure. For each, in the other. Their bodies were filled with smells and tastes of each other. Of the sensation of each other imprinted on them and the absolute comfort and intimacy of lying with each other and being aroused again and again, sometimes playfully, sometimes passionately, and sometimes with a mere touch.

When they woke, they would get ready and drive out of town to their favourite Dhaba- the roadside restaurants that the truckers and travelling folk frequented. This one was on the Western Express Highway, near Dahisar, on the way out of town towards the western ghats, the Sahayadri range of mountains that shield the Deccan plateau from the harshest of the monsoons. It was a Punjabi style cuisine which had all the specials of the makke-ki-roti (Corn breads) and sarson-ka-saag (mustard leaf curry) with the fresh blob of homemade butter on it, served with the traditional big glasses of fresh lassi (thick whipped buttermilk). They would eat to their heart's content. And like every time, not be able to finish the huge lassi portion, and like every time, resolve to request a single glass of lassi the next time. The moment they said this, as they shook their heads, as if trying to make a mental note of this, they would both catch each other's eye and burst out laughing. A sort of ritual of a joke. And still in the mirth, pay their bill and get back into the car for the drive back.

It was a time for magic. Their own special blend of magic.

They were cocooned in their own world. Where they both were the only ones and were most important to each other. A private one. One where only the two of them could be in. There was no talk or even thought of any other. This was their own time. Nothing else came close. Nothing else was in their thoughts.

And the days and weeks seemed to flow in an intense whirl of sensation. A touch, a lunge, a swing, anything could unleash the overpowering flow of unbridled deep passionate lovemaking.

Blink.

Shruti took a step back from the embrace and looked at Shekar. 'You look not so good,' she said.

'You don't either,' he said. 'I am on starvation diet'- the laughter rumbled in his chest and found an answer in hers- 'No ice cream', they said in unison, their laughter bubbling over into their own precious joke.

They hugged each other again, close, trying to absorb the other into their senses.

'How long are you here for?', she cautiously ventured.

'Three weeks'.

She hugged him tighter, as if she couldn't let him go.

He laughed louder and said, 'I can't come any closer, you know'.

She let him go at that and they both sat down on the sofa, still holding each other.

'Lets eat some dinner first. Then we can go to sleep. You must be tired after your flight, and it is really late in Singapore too.'

'Sounds good to me".

Once they ate, the tiredness swept over them. It had been too long without each other. They both were trying so hard to go through their days as normally as possible and giving their highest output at work all along, while keeping a tight rein on their emotions. Not an easy task at all.

Shruti and Shekar were truly missing each other enormously. This was the fatigue that they had not let themselves feel even, all these past days. This was the fatigue of their deep and intense love and longing for each other. This was the fatigue of their forced separation, which they both had now endured, and were together again. The fatigue of going through the days, being at the cutting edge of their productivity, giving the results they felt comfortable with, for they each had very high standards of how well their own work should look like, and that's what they aspired to, rather than just the brief that they were given.

Blink.

The lost feeling that had settled in, once the reality struck that they were indeed alone, at least for the foreseeable future. That they had no option that they could have taken up, one that was even feasible at all, one that let them protect their mutual need to be with each other, while keeping their careers flowing in the right directions too. The only ones they could come up with were one or the other giving up, and giving up things that matter to them, seriously and big time.

Shruti listened to heartbreak and love lost kind of poetry sung with the most pathetic and heart rending ethos. Shakeel Badayuni's masterpiece of a naat, in praise of the Prophet Mohammed.

Bekas pe karam kijiye sarkar e madina

Gardish me hai takdeer bhanvar me hai safina

Hai wakt madad aayiye bigdi ko banane

Poshida nahin aapse kuch dil ke fasaane

Zakhmon se bhara hai kisi majboor ka seena!

Have mercy on my wretched soul, Oh leader of the holy city of Madina

My fate is in a vicious cycle while my ark is in a whirlpool

The time for aid is here so do come to resolve my troubles

The tales of my heart are not hidden from you

The chest of this helpless devotee is riddled with injuries!

Was it such an undoable option, one may have thought. Was it that hard to stay together? After all, the two of them had found each other and had built this private world of theirs, in the middle of everything else that was going on around them and had kept that world protected for so long, had invested in it, to make it strong and thriving, built a strong wall around themselves that could not be breached by anyone. Would not any couple want to protect that. Going together to Singapore was a good option for staying together and continuing to build a life together.

So many couples had done that. So many couples who were professionals like themselves, took career decisions in turns as well. Once it was driven by one partner and another time by another. Shekar had said that too, in his persuasive speech. He said next time they had career choice or location options, they would be driven by her career choice options.

Shruti didn't agree to this, as she did not see it working. Forget the rock bottom traditional setup of society itself and including their own families, who, while they had no objection to her having a career, were clearly in unison on the staying together at all costs theme. To them, her career was a good one, but it was an "also" one. If she quit today, it would be tough, kind of, but nothing devastating that they would worry or loose any sleep over at all.

If that was Shekar, well, now you are talking. His job, prospects and future were the ones that determined, if they, as a couple, in the grand scheme of things, were doing well at all. His being in a secure position that needed to be protected at all times, reeked of sexism, clearly.

They were sure she was going to give up her job at any rate, and sometime soon. They were perhaps taking private odds and placing bets on when that would happen.

Marriage, children, logistics, social needs, the reasons were trivial, at best, and preposterous, at worst.

She couldn't consult anyone on this. Not with such views. It did not matter they were considered progressive, nor even that, in case of her parents, she had been educated by them and she, their daughter, had built her career brilliantly, with her hard work. She had achieved so much over the years, built herself an excellent reputation in the industry along the way. Were they not proud of her achievements. Yes, they were. Did they think she should continue working here. No, most definitely not, especially if Shekar was going to move. And he was moving up in his career, wasn't he? She had to quit and follow him, no question. There was no scope for discussion or variation of the common theme every opinion centred around. The requirements of the "keep your husband happy" side of people were always touting how much more successful she would be, if she went along with him and made her career there if she could- they would all be rooting for her, no doubt. But if she couldn't or even in a case where she chose not to, they would still call her the winner. They assured her of that, as if that was supposed to push her over to choose to go, in the go or stay lots that they all seemed to have drawn on her behalf. To go, of course.

Was it just their inability to see all that was at stake here? She had her marriage on one side and her career on the other. Career was perhaps shorter life spanned than her marriage, which was to be for life, at least, if not seven lifetimes, as the Indian belief went.

She could well have pulled the short straw if she went and that was not only not visible to anyone, but it also seemed like if it indeed was visible, it did not matter. Enough.

Shruti was all alone, isolated on an island. She felt cut off from everyone. She had tried to speak to colleague and friends in the hope that some new solution would come out and that would be to the best interests of both of them, not just Shekar. There was no one she could speak to, who felt she was losing as big as she saw herself possibly lose.

Shekar himself, in this instance, seemed to be a little biased towards her going rather than a balanced pros and cons approach, with the final call being hers and hers alone, as he usually was. It would be his call if the matter was a decision that affected his career.

To be completely fair though, in this case, the decision affected both of them.

There was no guarantee she would get a senior enough position in a bank in Singapore, for starters, she could see that. There was all the process of finding companies that needed someone of not only, her skill set, her experience, but also, liked her as a person, to fill that role. She was in too senior a position and so had to have all boxes checked really. All in all, seemed too many imponderables to her. Too many things in the balance there, while she had a completely full bag here. She loved her work, she was doing great, she was challenged every day, and every day she rose up to meet those challenges, beautifully and completely.

How could anyone just write off all that she was, she stood for, what she had fought for, what she had made with her own abilities, sometimes stretched to the limits as well, and earned with her incredibly hard work. Her precious life. Her precious career. Finance was her first love and to work in investment banking at the highest and most difficult level, in mergers and acquisitions, was a dream that was out of reach for many people, right from the word go even, for some. But she had done it. Brick by brick and it was all there and hers to keep.

Since there was no guarantee or surety that Shekar would like the role he was assigned, even though he had gone over it, and had had endless conversations with the team, both in India and in Singapore, they finally agreed that he would go to Singapore and she would follow, all things being agreeable, in six months time. Phew! And that, as they say, was that!

Blink.

There seemed no change, no let up rather, in how exciting her job here was. Every day was a huge bonus for her learning as well as giving back to the deals all that she could, and then some.

Shruti looked at Shekar sleeping deeply next to her. It was a peaceful moment, poignant, loaded with their mutual magic and she let it wash over her. She took deep breaths and with every breath, sent out a prayer of thanks.

She was so very grateful he had come over, suddenly though it seemed. It was perfect timing because she was just beginning to doubt herself somewhat.

Blink.

After going through the lows of separation from her beloved half, to pick herself together, was no easy task. To keep herself at the top of the game at work was perhaps the easier part. She would just be lost in the work so, for that time, she did not feel or remember anything of the outside world. She used to meet friends sometimes and go to plays or shows too. Those times were difficult but the moment she turned the key into the door at home, she was in pain. Shekar was everywhere. She could sense him, feel him and breathe his scent. Torture par catastrophe.

What could she do differently she wondered. Had she gone too far in seeking her own life and keeping her own life and achievement secure? Should she tone down and look for a non alpha engagement with her personal goals? Was she incapable of having a healthy relationship and a healthy career and just like so many, she too would give up the career for the marriage? Or had she grown into a self contained persona with a bubble around herself that wouldn't be breached anymore by the heart strings being pulled? Had she grown roots and then trimmed them herself so she couldn't feel the ground anymore, and so could just move on?

This growth in herself had also made her completely aware of herself as a person, the deep connections she made with her inner self as she meditated deeply, was such a strong life force, it gave her incredible positive energy and connected her with her surroundings, each feeding off the positive energies and blending them together into a powerful energy system. She felt the positive vibes as she went about her work and all aspects of her life. Places, people and settings even, gave her positive and negative energies, so she adjusted her receptivity, and hence was that much more capable of drawing everyone towards a positive outcome.

This was several steps beyond simply her technical knowledge and abilities that she had learnt at business school or honed since.

The word 'alienation' comes from a Latin word that means the condition of being an outsider to oneself. When and where did some of us become outsiders to ourselves? Alienation also lies at the root of many an illness, perhaps the cause of breakdown in many relationships.

As Otto Rank, the psychiatrist, said, "Loneliness is a part of self definition for the modern man."

He said loneliness is an issue we will have to face each time we cut ourselves off from our roots. He felt that, faced with the most violent time in history and technology that has the power to take over our lives, the day is not far off when we will have to face an alienation that would force us to define ourselves, taking us back to our roots.

Fifty Nobel Laureates were given this question at a conference, three decades ago, to reflect and find an answer over three days. "If man has really progressed and if so, how much?"

Some of the brightest minds of our time, asserted that man has progressed, but little only and true progress will only come when he learns to integrate science with art and spirituality. They also said that the enemy of man is his alienation from his own self and he will find healing in the wisdom of the ancients, especially the east. Today, when more and more people are living as single members in a household as compared to any other time in history, this message could not be more true.

Blink.

She, incredible though it may sound, felt she was standing alone and yet strongly connected to her environment, particularly to nature. This awakening of spirituality within her which came about simply through her deep meditations was giving her strong roots, she realised.

Shruti was filled with a radiance that could only be described as one coming from a realisation that was deep inside her. She was now peaceful. She was never alone. She could never be. And neither would Shekar be. As long as they felt they were connected, and reached for each other with the same feelings, their love would ride out the toughest wave.

There was nothing to drop everything and rush off to be together right now. She could work on her deals which were at various stages, while perhaps going over to look for opportunities to move to Singapore in the coming months. Perhaps they could spend a few short breaks together travelling the beautiful region. Shekar and Shruti setting up a home in Singapore would give them both a sense of home in both cities, for as long as necessary. Travel time between the two cities being so short, was a big help too. There wasn't a big jet lag or long haul to meet either.

Shruti sensed a calm coming from Shekar too. There was none of the agitation he was going through when they were discussing the move before he left. At the time, there was a real conflict in his mind, that was clear in his manner. He wanted her to come with him and he wanted her to succeed in her career. He never wanted her to give up anything for his sake.

Now, he seemed just content being here. How did that happen? She didn't know. Perhaps he would tell her when he woke up. Then again, it wasn't important, was it? The calm he seemed to exude was definitely from a peace of mind, and a clarity of thought. And that thought was seeming so similar to hers.

There, it was that simple. The question that had been playing at both of their minds, threatening to spill and yet each of them, not wanting to be the first to broach it, was quietened before it became a little sore point.

Shruti settled herself in bed, next to Shekar. As she wriggled herself to a comfortable position, he stirred and took her into his embrace. We are doing fine, he seemed to say. We don't need to do anything now, except spend time with each other, his arms holding her close, were telling her. You and I are together again, and we will make magic again, his heart beating in his chest, below her head, seemed to confirm. With a sigh, she too said yes, mentally.

They would have an excellent three weeks together and at the end, she would see him off well in time for his flight. What could they do tomorrow? A long drive maybe? Oh, and on another note, was there any ice cream in the fridge? Shruti drifted off before she got any further.

Growing up

Aise bhi gunehgaar hum ho nahi saktey, Ki aansoon-on se qabr teri dhho nahi saktey.

Aye khuda hain aazmaaishen teri qubool, Lekin ye kya ki lag ke gale ro nahi saktey!

By Kausar Munir

I cannot be so guilty that I cannot wash your grave with my tears.

Oh Lord, I accept your continued testing of me, but what a fate that I not hold you tight and cry my heart out even?

The wind was strong today. Seemed to threaten to blow everyone and everything off one's feet. The sort of howling through the wind tunnels and the swishing and whooshing meant so much of the huddled sort of walking, with quickened steps, with head bent forward and the rush to get to wherever one was going.

Raashi was not one to be on a different page. She too had her jacket on, zipped up, hood on, and head bent low-trying to keep the hood on top of her head.

Her mind was whirring in a completely different place though.

She had just come out of the house just wanting to get away from the air so thick with tension, she could have put a sheet and slept on it!!

It wasn't the first time for her. This coming out of the house in a state of mind that she did not know where she was going, just that she needed to be out on her own for a while.

There were the days she could shut herself out on the balcony their home had, but not today.

Try as she might, she felt overwhelmed by the whole older sister feeling. She didn't know it was a reasonably common occurrence for some parents to think their oldest is a grown up the day they have a second child-

And she had two younger siblings, a girl and a boy.

She couldn't remember what she felt when they were born- she was two and a half when they came along. Twins, boy and girl, but no real memories there.

She had some half cloudy and fuzzy ones that seemed to come and go like shutters opening and closing, or the lightening lighting up one scene and then another in rapid succession.

Like the time they kept crying and nothing Mum, or Granny or the Nanny could calm either of them down. They put them into the buggy finally and tried to rock them but they were having none of it. They just kept screaming as loud as they could. Raashi quietly got out her story book, stood in front of the buggy and kept reading to them.

Granny was like, what on earth are you doing. Just stop and go away. We will take care of these two.

But she kept on. Mum was very proud of her that day, she remembered.

And the time her sister jumped off the ledge after her and landed smack on her face, her nose smashed up and there was blood everywhere. Mum asked Raashi to bring the ice and stay close to assist her. She had always thought Mum was super cool in such circumstances but Mum told her some time back that she was always impressed with how calm and collected Raashi was.

What had possibly happened in these years, to make things so very tense at home, that she came rushing out of there, time and again, and every time she resolved to move to the university as soon as she finished her A Levels, and make sure she would pick one that was not close to home.

For sure. It was important to know, wasn't it?

As the years rolled by, the experiences seemed to all blur out into each other. Raashi felt she was constantly asked to do things for others, without any commas or fullstops to this doing. It wasn't like she wasn't a helpful sort but it was all too much to drop things in an instant and be off helping out with something the person could very well do on their own steam, if they bothered to get their act together and move their butts, in the first plaee. What was it they say about asking for help- its always way easier, isn't it? The constant rubbing each other the wrong way began to show, hurt and interfere seriously onto her happiness.

Was it that matters really came to a head when Auntie Augusta came along one day and set herself up in the guest room? She was only supposed to be staying over for a few days while she waited for her pension papers to be got into order, but she hung on for simply ages. It always seemed like the wrong time to leave.

Like her habit of praying before she left the house and then going to the toilet before she actually left. Then she would come and pray at the altar again, since she's been to the toilet, and once she prayed, she would have to go to the toilet before she left. It was simply the last thing she did before she left home. And now that she went to the toilet, it wouldn't be respectful to not pray before she left home. And so it went on. Endlessy.

There was one time when she was actually going to church and with this to-ing and fro-ing, the church already shut for lunch by the time she got there.

No wonder she was a permanent sort of resident, never leaving their home.

And she was trouble with all the capital letters. She was their Father's relative, so Mum was a bit on the back foot, so she made Mum run circles around her. Always wanting this or that. She told her tales about the kids "misbehaving" and how she was so "concerned" for Mum. Initially, she fell for Auntie's tricks and used to give them earfuls, and they saw Auntie grinning smugly. Soon Mum too saw through this but couldn't do anything about it. Not without speaking to their Father first. And he was travelling for work. The home became unbearable and everyone became short with everyone else. Raashi couldn't handle the pressure any more. Her exams were tough enough and she always looked forward to the peace of her home and the bliss of her room. But Auntie would station herself there at anytime and begin making demands. Raashi was just a young girl, and not in complete control of her temper always. Particularly during her exams. Her Mum used to try to deflect most of Auntie and her barbs but she couldn't watch and guard all the time. There was a multitude of tasks to do and some were away from home as well.

Auntie would stop at nothing. The servants were spies and ruthlessly prodded into telling tales and constantly questioned. Age old rumours were thrown into the air with such finesse that if the person wasn't expecting trouble and lots of it as well, they would be gasping for air very soon.

Because she had the sort of status of a kind of mother in law, that too, in a reasonably conservative family, who were respectful towards elders, it was her dream setting.

She set out meddling into everything. Whether it was Raashi's parents stuff or hers' or her siblings'. Nothing was out of bounds it would seem. And if they were successful in explaining away any point raised or in deflecting a hard ball bowled in their direction, she would just go off and come up with new stuff to throw at them. Ingenuity of the wrong kind in full free flow.

While everyone in the family couldn't wait for Father's return, tempers were frayed.

The last straw seemed to snap when Auntie invited her whole family over for a get together at home, Raashi's home. And without even asking her Mum. Mum was furious. She kept a hold on herself, and now, Mum and kids put their heads together to deal with this grown menace. They resolved to keep to themselves, not speak much, and not offer any help. If help was asked for even, they would each act busy and back each other up if necessary to stay busy.

It wasn't the easiest thing to do- battle of wills pitted against Auntie Augusta, the grand dame in the art of manipulation.

So let the games begin they thought.

It was all systems go from the start. They had to be especially on guard all the time and not let a single moment of laxity come to pass. No relaxing and thinking it is all clear. Auntie was so good at pitting one against the other, that before they knew it the children would be fighting with each other, or trying to explain rumours, which had no basis at all.

It could be anything really. You were meeting someone in the park, were you not, or, why is your bedroom light on at 11 pm, or, what happened to you the other day-who's the boy you came home with? It was like rapid fire machine guns going at full blast.

Who had the stomach for this sort of filth day after day, leave alone the patience. And above all to be polite and cover for each other with credible sounding responses, because respond you must!

What kind of person would spend their lives winding other people up, interfering in their lives, with zero provocation, regardless of the fact that they were, in fact, being so helpful? What sort of perverted mind could turn mother against child and siblings against each other and sit around to watch the fun. For entertainment?

Auntie had a brain like a geiger counter, continuously ticking and finding new ways around closed doors. She was relentless. And they had to play dumb too, so Mum wouldn't get into any trouble for playing games with a mother in law figure. It would be really big trouble if her real mother in law heard of it.

The days passed slowly and with her exams going on, Raashi has no patience or time with these machinations. She found her siblings lack of patience trying as well. They began to argue and fight over simple things, like whose idea they should try next, or what should they eat even!

Were there not any more important things in the world to do?

Surely someone could come out and tell the woman she was way out of line!

Try as she might she couldn't put these troubles out of her head. She took a deep breath one day and decided to just focus on the studies.

Her Father came back and it seemed the sun was beginning to shine again. The clouds had indeed parted. Auntie Augusta was on her best behaviour, but it was too late. Already, Father was furious that she was still 'in residence', when she should have gone long ago, and once he heard the story from his family, his rage knew no bounds. The very next day he spoke to his Auntie and told her they all had to go away soon and booked her on the train to her home, leaving the very next day.

And that, as they say, was that. He took her with all care to board the train and said goodbye. To their credit they never let her come near their home again, nor did they ever speak to her again either. It was quite a deep and hurtful experience for the family to go through.

Raashi wondered if it wouldn't have been better to not let her walk all over them in the first place? Would her grandmother really not understand this rubbish that was going on in the name of taking some help? Were relationships so fragile between a daughter in law and her husband's family that she had to endure and because she did, her children too?

213

What kind of social straightjacket was her mother in anyway. Even after so many years of marriage and a girl ready for university, nearly. The whole thing seemed so wrong. And her father too had to tread lightly. There was no asking her what the hell she was trying kind of thing. Rather smile and be very nice to her. How could that be right?

And her Mum was a strong woman, she knew that. She was still bound in so many trivialities which shackled her like antediluvian ideas of respectful behaviour. She always let them question and rustle up the waters on any subject. The change was coming. And Raashi and her siblings were the first generation for bringing this about.

Raashi was energised by this thought and much heartened too. All in all though the whole episode of Auntie Augusta and her siblings pulling and stretching her nerves was too much for Raashi. She still ended up picking the university that was further away than the one that was near. She couldn't wait to get away from home, it would seem.

The days of preparation seemed to crawl by and finally it was time. Bags packed and loaded, she was ready to leave. She thought she had it all quite well in hand when she said a breezy goodbye to both siblings and with a bit of hesitation on her part, and her Father was done too.

"Here is a note for you, my dear," said Mum, putting the envelope into her hands. "I do hope you enjoy every moment of your growing up and every moment of campus life. Student days at university are the best days of learning and just learning, along with so much fun you have with your friends. Be happy. Stay safe and do call or come over if you feel like. Anytime." And Mum gave her a big, warm Mum special hug.

Somehow tears seemed to push at her eyelids, trying to wriggle their way out and even with her rapid blinking, some of them streaked away across her cheeks, like fast getaway cars.

She settled herself in her seat on the plane and with trembling fingers, opened the letter and started to read the pages that were closely written in her mother's clear writing. Mum wrote just the way she spoke, she registered subconsciously.

My darling Raashi

I've been wanting to have a long chat with you for a long time- somehow I felt you would understand.

For me, finance and financial markets in all its aspects has always been my first love. I was so involved in my work I never paused to think how it would change when we would have our children.

Initially we were way too busy and then we were way too busy and way too stressed, so conception was perhaps more difficult than taking a walk in space. So fourteen years after marriage is when we finally made it to becoming expectant parents!!

Once pregnant, I was still at work, and the sheer miracle of it began to sink in slowly. One day, there I was, sitting in a meeting advising clients on the acquisition of a company, and in me, there is this embryo breathing and growing, cells multiplying at enormous speed. Then it was the baby itself. Given the lateness of our parenthood, I must have been the most tested mum to be, or at least among the most tested. Protein levels, hormone levels, intake levels- you name it. At every test, the nurse, the doctor and even the receptionist seemed to think I needed to be given the lesson on the importance of the various levels being maintained, enhanced, reduced, taken care of in all the ways they were continually telling me. At some point I felt like the imbecile I must have looked... Oh, the look their faces when they would look at the reading and say, hmmm, protein level is borderline. If this goes x points down, you have to take only bed rest!!

I lived in more than a bit of trepidation at the thought of each approaching test.

As I continued through my weeks of pregnancy, I became more aware of the reality of social pressure around me too- it had been there for me to produce the children for ages, since I got married actually. Everyone older was always assessing my child bearing capabilities and what the chances of my announcing a pregnancy were or the potential reasons for my handing in the towel, quitting my precious investment banking job, so to speak. I was constantly reminded of the raw material all being in place and all it needed for me was to go and conceive. If that didn't sound gross enough, I don't know what did.

But now that I had made that grade, it was more specific- would it be a boy or a girl? Right from the shape of my tummy to the way I stood, sat, lay down or walked were assessed and I was living a nightmare.

While the doctor in London said he wouldn't tell me whether I had a boy or girl, at my 16 week scan, I remember going to the hospital in Moscow- I was there anyway for a couple of weeks for a 'nearly done deal' kind of client discussion. I wasn't going to pass up on that one now, was I, pregnant or not!

Being a teaching hospital the doctor had a bunch of students around to explain things to- he looked at the scan and then stopped. He came close to me lying on the bed and said, do you know what you are having? I said no- he asked, do you want to know? I said, yes. He said its a girl and it's the most beautiful thing you can have.

That stayed with me-

In spite of social pressure on the first born to be a son or have a son anyway- I prayed I would love this child for itself, boy or girl.

We see the state most girls end up in- they are raised to think, use their judgement and told they can go and achieve whatever they want, and then they see, all around them, people trying to slot them into boxes- the nerd, the hottie, the party type and all the rest. In addition to all the compromises they end up making, in the name of relationships or career or whatever. Or they simply give up, even if they have fought hard and struggled hugely and against all odds, to learn, achieve and maintain their job status. However difficult it was for them to achieve, and achieve it they have, with their own sheer hard work. Just to conform or to "not rock the boat".

Girls learn quickly to be who they are expected to be and behave how they are expected to-

Who they are and what they think and what they want to do remains buried sometimes so deep within- they themselves forget who they are and what they are capable of.

This is what I was up against- this is the mould I promised myself I will break. Not because I have been discriminated against or I have compromised, but because my children are starting on a clean slate and this would only be fair for them!!

I wanted my child, my girl to have siblings for sure. In spite of every advice that I was possibly too old, I did it.

I do feel the three of you are a complete team. And wondrously, you are all similar in nature, kind and concerned as well as curious, enthusiastic, eager and above all brilliantly clever.

You are all high energy, which means I could do nothing else when you were awake and younger and now, perhaps a bit of my work when you are around.

As is my habit with something I don't know much about, I started to learn and for that, to read extensively, discuss with others, watch videos, on the subject of children, parenting, even marital relationships when children arrive and family settings with children- you name it!! This acquiring of knowledge on the subject continues, as a matter of fact- anything on the subject.

You are all curious how people's lives work and why some people are more privileged than others or less so.

Consciously, I thought the best thing is to let you evolve their own sense of judgement of fairness and right or wrong. It would be too unfair and too unlike me as well, to pass any of the insecurities on the grounds of gender or such without you seeing a situation first, that makes you aware of the practice and then you question it.

So at any time, unless it's a dangerous situation where someone could get hurt, I describe what has happened to each of you, and ask you what you would do to resolve the dispute or share the chocolate or share the game- play it differently.

I have been very forceful, however, to condemn, in the strongest possible way, even the thought of any competition between you. I find that children who compete with each other in say, even games, continue to carry that over into competing with each other in everything and that affects how they interact with each other. They see even the most unrelated and obscure things as a way of scoring points over each other or as a plot for the others to score over them.

I encourage you to compete against yourselves, look at what you lost and what you did well, so you can hone the good and rework the not working. The end we are trying to achieve is always to better yourselves-excel in your own education, for yourselves, and to play competitive sport as well, to win. Win I define as doing your best and nothing less than that. Doing your absolute best and focusing on the quality of your effort at all times and honing it meticulously, and not on the result here, whatever it may be. It takes great practice to make yourself a doer like it says in the Bhagavat Gita. One who concentrates on the effort and not the result, because if the effort has been made in the right way and at the right time, the result is inevitable perhaps. I am not being simplistic and choosing not to see what we are up against and what you as children of the millennium, are going to be up against. You will be able to stay confident and take the steps with fortitude and courage without letting fears hold you back. Which for me, is a losers option. To say I am fearful and hence will not act.

You have learnt to regroup and build yourself up again when you lose- and learn from it- in sport it would be what made you get the points when you won, and what made you make the mistakes that you lost points on. Typically, when fencing, you could come back from being down 1-4 to win the match, sometimes handsomely and at other times, by a single hard-fought point.

And that hairs breadth is just the difference between win and lose, all along life. We are just so close to losing it all, when we make a move and gain all of it back and more. Until the next challenge comes along. Just like, as Swami Vivekananda said, darkness is just nothing but an absence of light, life is not a bed of roses, but one with roses and thorns too. After all, the rose bush has plenty of thorns along with blooms.

We just need sufficient tools in our toolbox to go through both happy and tough times. That is just all what growing up is all about - making a toolbox full of tools strong enough and varied enough to let you face any situation in your life, and face it with confidence.

When you were still living at home, I tried and encouraged you to concentrate on the work or the play and showed you how the result varies when you concentrate or not, whether you concentrate hard and at your best, or not, whether you use the tools in your toolkit or not. I did it even at the dinner table- I showed you how much you would enjoy a meal with an amusing conversation or appreciation for the food, rather than a fuss or a tantrum!!

To be honest, there was a time when I thought it would not be a good idea to have a girl child at all- the world I lived in would perhaps mercilessly squash her before she even really reached out and spread her wings.

There are times even now when I seriously fear for the safety or innocence of my children- now I could worry for the boy as well- these concerns perhaps will fade as you grow stronger and more capable or just over time...

In many ways too, I think, your world is better- you have enormous exposure- you are comfortable in your own skins- I encourage you to be proud of who you are, love yourselves as well. Be your own best friend. Make sure you treat yourselves with the utmost respect, the same as you would expect others to treat you with, and not only because of what you can do or what rank you can get in a contest, but simply because you are who you are. Without judgement.

You have the relationship with me in which, I am constantly reiterating everyday, subtly or directly, that I am here for you to ask questions or even if you feel you might have possibly gotten into a situation that you are not going to like or may need help- you can talk to me about how you feel, at any time.

In fact I have done this so often with you that you can pretend I am there with you and have the conversation you would have had with me and get to the answer or solution, all on your own.

I am merely the sounding board for your thinking until you have the strength to think through issues for yourself and resolve them too, step by step, in a methodical, meticulous and complete manner.

Particularly for you three, since you are all always on the back foot, as far as talking about what you feel is concerned- it's been a slow encouragement process to make you understand that you can talk to me as if you are talking to yourself and coming up with the ideas for going forward, seemingly from your own heads.

You never have had the inhibited childhood where children were not really encouraged to ask any question they liked or talk about something they saw or felt, openly. Children should be seen and not heard? Really?

In comparison, we, dear Raashi, had a very insulated childhood and nothing to prepare us for independent life except when we were actually living it. I remember going to give in my form for my post graduate degree, no less, and not knowing what a pay order looked like. The clerk at the office laughed long and hard at me, asking if I was sure I was a graduate. I had attached the bank receipt of payment instead. How could I have known that after they issue a receipt for payment, the bank would make out a pay order, which, by the way, says pay order, at the top and looks far more formal than that little receipt ! Thats how I learnt though. On the job, with many misses than hits.

I don't know about kickass, but I think you have learnt to do the right thing, use your initiative and show restraint in difficult situations and enthusiasm to help- work hard, play hard!!

You have learnt about families and friends, of relationships, of jealousies, of bullies and of happy times when friends come back across countries and are desperate to meet you. You learnt to reach out and make the effort to touch other people's lives, to make them happy, especially special people like grandparents.

It's a fantastic journey, your life, and I hope I have been able to help you collect the tools to work your way through, and have loads of fun on their way!!!

Lots of love to you,

Mum.

Raashi was simply overwhelmed with the tears that she let flow freely this time.

She thought- "Oh Mum!. My dear lovely precious Mum. How well you know me. How much effort you have taken to know me and give me all that I need to have as tools for my life. And reading your letter, all my battles and endless pushing and pulling with my brother and sister seem so mindless and needless, actually. You are so right, and I have been so foolish. I wish I could turn the plane back and come and hug you once more, but I will come in the term break and do just that. I will also share this with my brother and sister. It is time for new beginnings all around. We may all yet have many moments of time spent happily and with a respect to share and after all, isn't that what I am supposed to have learnt too, from the master teacher, among us all, you?"

The peace that descended on Raashi was more than worth its weight in pure unadulterated, glistening gold. She felt still and encompassed in the warm glow of knowing and in an instant, understanding what she felt and why. There were no dark clouds anymore. No hesitation to figure out how to moon over the thought that she had no one even in her own family who understood her a little and had the proverbial hand always extended towards her in the friendship, laced with deep and complete respect that she always craved.

It was such a moving yet powerfully stabilising thought for her to now know she was safe, secure and mentally fully supported. The thought sent warm goosebumps down her arms. She rubbed them happily. Now she would go do her brand new university education and come the term break, it would certainly be home time.

There was so much she was going to talk to her Mum and Dad about and so much she wanted to share with her siblings too.

Life was going to be good!!

Roots

Kabhi yun bhi aa meri aankh me ke meri nazar ko khabar na ho- mujhe ek raat navaaz de magar uske baad seher na ho

Maybe you will come sometime into my eyes, such that even I won't notice you coming by, just for one night you come and adorn me so, but I hope that night never has a dawn!

Aurora quickly grabbed the scarves from the lower shelf in her cupboard, pushed the drawers shut and the doors too, took one huge step to the suitcase open on the stool at the foot of her bed. In one easy, practised move, the scarves were in and with one final look she knew the suitcase was ready to close up. Then came the cream jar for her hand bag - she always thought of the cream jar first and somehow it seemed to always be the last one in, whenever she packed and it didn't seem to make any difference whether she had time to pack or it was one of those rushed trips…

There, that was put in and too and now she was ready to leave for the station. The bag with her water and a little bunch of snacks was waiting on the table in the hallway. She liked to keep a few treats for the journey, whether by air, train or road. Something about the childhood surely was there. They always had some special snacks at some special stops and over the years, even when she and her siblings were older, they all were so used to those, and they still looked forward to them with all the eager enthusiasm of a much younger child. The eager anticipation of the train pulling into the junction meant a little extra halt time and the chance to get at those fresh black berries or spicy potato fritters or even the altime hit, the flavoured milk. This was long before to-the-moon and back long lists of flavours for milk shakes became the norm. Any shop with less than twenty-five flavours was a total not really a good one nowadays! But those days were different. Even one single cardamom flavour in a tiny 150 ml bottle of milk had a piece of real heaven right there.

Somehow, every time she travelled it was a replay of a bit of that kind of journey so she kept some of her favourite snacks to munch along, a few types of snack just to cover all bases, a good book and one of her lovely meals too. Just in case-it was a time tested just in case-just in case the food was not on time, or it was not to her taste.

She was a very seasoned traveller, no surprise there. She was an architect and a very successful one at that. She was always in demand for a project that "had to have her expertise" or for a conference where the people organising were "sure she was the one, and the only one, who could give the attendees that extra bit of knowledge or nuance from her vast and varied experience. She was like gold dust to them. Having her on the list was precious and ensured not only the attendance of so many other bit of fuss kind of architects, but ensured the success of the meeting too.

She absolutely loved her job, but this journey was different.

But first she needed to say good bye to Armaan. He was waiting for her outside, pacing with meticulous steps and trying so hard to seem like it was not a couple of weeks she was going away for, but just a morning-evening kind of trip for work.

He was a man of a huge number of words, and loved to use them at any opportunity to talk, especially to Aurora. Talk about anything and everything. He and Aurora could talk for hours, days and weeks without feeling the strain of it ever being remotely like, too much at all. That was how well tuned they were, to each other. That was the effect they had on each other. She brought out the best in him and he did the same for her.

What had started off as a very wary acknowledgement of each other, on a holiday, grew into this wonderful intertwined life, so filled with thoughts from each other being shared and moments full of caring, it was a dream.

It was a cruise on the mediterranean, actually, that they met. They were on doing the same excursions, as they made their way from Istanbul, with all the stops on the way, right up to Venice, over three full weeks. They were in the same groups and it was apparent early on that they had the same interests- everything about the centuries old civilisations laid out in front of them by their guides was

Lata Gullapalli

a fascinating spread, and one which they eagerly took in. Soon enough they were sharing smiles and looks and then fell into a conversation, one that never stopped.

Armaan came from a very 'we are all friends- really close friends' kind of family. Everyone laughed and joked with each other and somehow things which needed to be done were done, and, with so much merriment in the air, it was hard to be alone or left alone at any time. It was such a complete togetherness and incessantly talking about what they thought, or felt, about any issue. As far as he could recall, he was asked what he thought about what was being discussed, and what he would like to do, if it pertained more to him, or what they should all do, if it was a family one.

They all approached any problem the same way. They set aside all the jokes and sat around a table and talked about the matter, sometimes over days, until they were all satisfied that the various aspects, permutations, combinations have been discussed. And a mode of action that was the right one, picked up, picked through at length and pronounced good enough to go.

And over the next few weeks, or as long as was necessary, the others would closely follow the developments and keep close tabs on what was going on.

There was never any hint of anyone being remotely judgemental or flaunting an ego, in any of this. All Is, Ids and egos were left clearly outside the door when it came to family.

If it was something to celebrate too, they came together like no other. They talked about the achievements, paid fulsome compliments and made little gestures to show they cared- that was all that anyone could ask for really. It wasn't the right thing to make a huge show and noise for any achievement. A quiet hug and a kind word were so much more well meant and respectfully given and taken.

For all his life, Armaan could only remember how he rushed to his family whenever he had good or bad news, whenever he wanted to share anything at all, for that matter. They all felt the same way. The whole atmosphere at home was a very positively charged one. The feeling of an enveloping warmth filled with a trusting affection, was a powerful trusting cocoon to be living in. For anyone.

And that's what he felt was the least anyone was entitled to, simply by being part of a family unit. Not for what they brought to the relationship or what they could do for others- that would be an insulting idea, in the extreme.

Any visitor entering their home always commented on the absolute warmth they felt upon entering the house. His mother always said it was because she did some intense meditation and practiced her singing classical songs and hymns, at every opportunity.

Her mediation was so powerful, she could feel the goodness and warmth come flowing into her home and spread everywhere. Even her music teacher commented on how much more powerful their singing and recitations were here, in her home. The presence of the divine was somehow palpable.

Perhaps it was that, and perhaps it was the strong bonds they had built with each other.

It wasn't like they didn't disagree. Oh no, not at all. As siblings, they disagreed a lot, especially as children, and they could be and were very very vocal about their ideas too. But there was always a decency in their speaking to each other, a respect in never crossing the undrawn and unwritten lines of how, even in the deepest of disagreements with each other, they had a real deep respect for each other and an absolute magic of all encompassing love.

Aurora's case was different.

She shrugged into her coat and went to say good bye to Armaan. He held her close. It felt like heaven, the sheer warmth of his embrace. The reassurance that he was indeed with her, and understood her apprehension at this upcoming journey. She let her head rest against his deep barrel of a chest, one that was her refuge many a time and a very welcoming one, for sure.

Every day, every moment, she felt the gratitude flow through her, for having found Armaan and been with him for so many years.

He had been most patient with her too. For that she was doubly grateful. Initially, it was perhaps the logical step to spend time together and when that was going well, to move in together. And when that went along for some time with great results, to think of a legal named relationship.

It was usually the case, but not for Aurora. She took her time settling in with Armaan, she began to relax in the relationship really slowly, almost to the point where he felt it was slower than the snail pace. It was so difficult for him since he was used to such rich and well intended bonds of family and relatives all his life. He could not understand her reluctance to having anything legally binding. She seemed happy enough with the living together part of it. He felt very insecure in the beginning. It would seem like she had her foot stuck in the door, ready to leave at any moment.

Gradually, he began to understand that it was not him at any fault, rather her own fears that didn't give her the confidence, even when he was so clearly reassuring. He accepted that she would only commit another level if he let her go, so to speak. And he was so sure, that Aurora was indeed the one woman he would roam to the ends of the earth with, without any question, he went with her idea of just living together. That was some twelve years ago and counting.

To his credit and his credit alone, he never insisted she played any of the long time partner roles by his side. He always left it to her choice. She did come along sometimes and sometimes she did not. He was indeed a man in a million, or several millions blessed as he was, with such empathy and understanding, that he dealt with her many an occasion, with the utmost gentleness.

Aurora was so sure that it was only okay for them to live together and nothing was in their life that imposed any structure or binding, legally.

She was now invited to her brother's daughter's engagement ceremony, to be held over three days and to which everyone in the family was coming to. And everyone was planning to stay for two weeks to catch up.

She had long resisted being in touch with her family. Her decision to move to a city at the other end of the country for her studies was the perfect excuse to leave her family home. She was offered a full scholarship with a research assistantship so it was a golden break, one she took with both hands.

So why go now? It was Armaan who insisted she go. It was way overdue he said. She needed to go and meet her family. She needed to go over the past and make the peace with herself. She needed to let all the thoughts go so she would be fully healed, otherwise there was always a part of her holding back. He was so right. The memories of the past, however dull or at the back of her mind she thought they were, were, in fact, not so far away. She could never help herself from the flashes of time that came totally unbidden into her present, just to give her a comparison. And that was not pleasant. She had to fight the thoughts, the memories from taking over and washing her into the waters of depression, churning her insides till she felt herself bend and give in.

Maybe he was right.

Goodbye said, and a load of stay safe on the train, eat and drink properly, wish I was going with you and watch your luggage, enjoy your trip, have an open mind, she stepped into the taxi and was off to the train station. Checking in with the conductor and was installed into her cabin for the long journey. Two nights and a whole day to get to her parent's home. "Dinner was being served in the dining car, Madam", the conductor told her.

She looked around at the familiar setting of the sleeper cabin, with the long windows and bed made up with the crisp sheets. It was one of her favourite pastimes, to lie in bed and gaze out of the window of the moving train. The stations that were halts during the night and the star-studded pollution free country side and the train speeding through it all. The buzz of excitement went through her! She took off her coat and scarf, unpacked her basics and with a check of her appearance, made her way to the dining car.

It was such a pretty room. Tables with white linen and polished flatware place settings. Long windows with little curtains, tied back. And a stunning glass ceiling to complete the view.

Aurora sat down and took a look at the menu. Another promising dinner. Loads of favourites, starting with a cypress salad and her caramel custard to finish.

For Aurora, it was a first that Armaan asked her what she wanted to do, on everything. As far as she could recall, except her birthday flowers, there was nothing he did not ask her first about what she would like, or prefer, or think of.

Never had anyone asked her what she thought or what she felt about anything. She was the oldest child and for as long as she could remember of her childhood, she was to be the responsible one and either she was following orders or she was in charge of making sure the younger ones were following orders.

Never had her parents asked her what she felt about anything really, and if they did, on the rare occasion, it was only to brush it aside in the most patronising of tones, saying, of course you couldn't be expected to know anything, leave alone have a balanced opinion. Relatives seemed to be in the same mould so she didn't see any other way of thinking all her growing up years.

In all the taking care of her siblings and being responsible herself, she was already grown into a young woman, lovely though she was, in every way, she was totally unaware of it. Never had anyone in her family ever appreciated her goodness, her kindness or the numerous brilliant things she was capable of. Most of all, she was not sure she was loved for just being there. For being a part of the family she cared so much about. It seemed so much like a need based relationship.

After so many years of being the troubleshooter and part of the background, even pushed around by her parents' relatives who considered it okay to criticise her way of speaking, manner of dressing, choice of subjects at college, you name it, virtually, she was completely fed up and tearing her hair out, almost daily. Never had her parents stepped in to support her. It didn't have to be verbal even. Sometimes a look, or an arm around her shoulders would have been more than enough, to do the job. A kind glance or a gentle hand on hers would have done the work of a million care balms to soothe her agonised feelings and ones which had begun to take on the task of chipping away at her feeling of self worth, with alarming regularity.

She was so innocent in her affection for her family, she truly believed it when, she was told that parents don't praise their children, so the children have their feet on the ground and not in the clouds. Parents believing children can do no wrong, or, that parents take care not to support their children in front of others, so it doesn't look disrespectful or needlessly arrogant, on their part.

Over time the standard stack of excuses she pulled some out from to explain their behaviour, or lack of it, seemed to have also lost their lustre, and she would herself end the thought with the "couldn't they have spoken in my favour just this once?" And she always had no answer to give.

Why was there such a dichotomy between the reactions she brought out at home and those she was swept away with, outside? Her friends or their parents, sometimes even strangers, had no problem showering praise, blessing, favours and so much more, she felt even more empty when she came home. The maximum she got even when she narrated those stories was a "hmmm."

The list of responsibilities seemed to be long and intense, so much so, she began to feel the pressure of being at home close in on her. While she loved her family to bits and was so proud of them and their work, play, all their achievements and without reserve, why was she so isolated from a good word or a pat on the back, a state so bereft of the warm reciprocal affection?

She had to get out of there. Even this idea wasn't hers. She would never have thought of it. It came when her classmates were discussing next steps at the college, at one of the canteen coffee chats. Everyone was talking about going out of home and the amazing things they would all do, some would live it up and others would live it up even more. Everyone agreed it would be a huge experience to be out of their families' sphere of influence. And one they were desperate to find out what it really felt like.

Listening to them Aurora found a seed of an idea planted in her, and as the days went by, she herself was amazed at how calmly and clearly she put the fact before her family that she has taken a place at a university about 900 miles away, to study architecture. And earned the place with a scholarship so she didn't need her parents to be spending any money on her education any more, either. They were very shocked and refused to discuss it at the beginning since they felt there could be no conversation on her going away from home for university. After all, there were good ones right in their city, were there not? But she did not engage at all, and they seemed to get the idea that she really was keen on the course and the location of the university. It still did not seem an idea that she wanted to leave her home.

That's how she stepped out of her home for the first time. And never went back since to stay at home again. She did go back in the initial years for a few days at a time, but these visits did not register in her the warmth she sought. So she began to make excuses. Simple ones at first, and feeling a pile of guilt when she made them, but again, over time, she was amazed at how adept she became in anticipating the invite and evading it, yet again.

Until now, that is. This time it was mostly Armaan, but she seemed open to making this journey too.

Meal done, she walked back to her sleeper carriage and settled into the freshly made bed, nestling close to the window. The night was dark in front of her but the sky had stars splayed so beautifully across, enormous numbers of glittering little jewels, made so clearly visible by the pollution free country air, it was simply breathtaking.

There was something about the swaying motion of the train, the telegraph poles whizzing past, the clicking of the train going over the track joints, that made for trips down memory lane. The mind switched into the past and brought the images vividly outside her window, as if they were just happening. She was so gently eased into the what was done, she let the images go over without resistance.

The million images of her being pushed aside, neglected and passed over and all the rest of the hurtful instances, as she remembered them, came rushing through as water through a pipe once the tap has been opened to the fullest.

This time was different though. As she sat there and let the past relive itself in any form it liked, today there came several million more of the memories of what her parents taught her and her siblings. How they all lived, laughed at mealtimes and travelled together, all came in a kaleidoscope of vivid rich colours, and warm in their hues.

What a way to parent as hers did? What a way to teach. The child has fun as well, and the lesson has been learnt too. Right where they are. What they taught, not as a lesson or even as a moral of a story or incident, but as a way of life. They taught them through what they said and did, and how they lived every moment of their days as examples.

Of the way they used to particularly dress for each time of the day, meticulously. And how they used to dress for every occasion suitably. How they spoke to all those different people that came to their home. To friends, to strangers, to relatives both older and younger, to people who came to ask for help, even acquaintances or distant family who needed to stay over before continuing on their journeys to elsewhere- needless to say, who couldn't afford hotel stays.

How they spoke when they visited other peoples homes or went to the ritual "dine out" for birthdays. How they sat, used the napkins, the cutlery and all the rest of it.

This was the personal appearance aspect. Then there was the mind being fed too. Music played at home daily, at different times was different music. The children were given lessons in music and dance. The visits to concerts, movies and theatricals were an outing which was to be savoured and imbibed, clearly. Visits to the libraries where they could choose their own books and read them. What luck! They read voraciously. One vacation they read about nine books a day. What a treat!

Hosting was a fine art. Right from setting the home and putting out new table and bed linen, to purchasing fresh vegetables and fruit was down to a fine order that backed beautifully into the arrival of the guests, whether they were coming just for dinner or staying over. Menus were planned, ice put to set, little bites prepared for the drinks that would be offered.

As she grew older, Aurora did come to doing many of these on her own- that was just a way of learning being organised and so avoiding hitches when the event came along. She remembered finishing her studies for that time in advance so she wouldn't lose time.

People came for advice and help so often, they were treated with the same respect as any household member. The refreshments were always offered- even if it meant running quickly to the store nearby for a packet of savoury snack or biscuits in case some couldn't be prepared at home.

The immense travel they did, almost the length and breadth of the country. Not only did they go to some of the most amazing places and stay in some of the most gorgeous guest houses, they went around and explored those places. They went around and saw the historical sights and did the local treks and tasted the local food too. Eaten in the local way.

The love for buildings and architecture was born somewhere between seeing ancient temples or ruins of universities and some marvels that had stood the tests of time as well as invasions.

How her parents put others before themselves. They embodied the service before the self.

When they had the pandemic when she was fifteen, how, her Mother, even though she was an early patient of the disease and seriously weakened by it, went about preparing personal protective equipment at home, and in sewing groups. How she prepared from scratch, meals for the hospitals and supplied them. For months on end. And kept other volunteering work going too, making calls, delivering medicines. It was, she said, because, we must have the humanity to help others as much as we can. Simply because they need help and we can.

Not only this, so many times she had seen her Mother help hugely, people who were critical of her earlier or even sometimes perhaps a bit stuffy and rude.

Her Mother just smiled and moved on.

Was it any wonder she was at home in an instant wherever she went and could eat a sampling of most food placed in front of her, provided it was vegetarian, that being the only caveat!

Or that she could speak a smattering of most languages within hours and sometimes just minutes of arriving at a place thousands of miles from home.

That she was the first in the list for running a plan of action by, somehow she seemed to know the order to do things in, working backwards from the endpoint.

Or even that she was the first person most of her friends and even acquaintances called when they needed help or advice. And it seemed to sit lightly on her too. She helped and advised and didn't give it another thought.

Helped and advised because she could. Even made time for it many times.

Where were all these immense treasures before? Where had her mind hidden them?

The constant battle she had was with her not being able to voice her thought or feeling. She felt she was ready to participate in a discussion.

But perhaps her parents felt she wasn't ready and needed to learn some more? Perhaps they wanted her to observe them some more and to hone her skills some make before she ventured in that direction.

Perhaps even the push that seemed to shove her over the edge and make her take the decision to leave home on her own was their way of getting her started on her journey, now that they felt she was ready?

This was all so new, this thought that it was all part of their being firm in making her understand all that they, and not she, felt she needed to know before making any move in the direction of independent life.

Why could she not see it before or even feel it, even when Armaan repeatedly asked her to try going back to see her parents? She had been just closed to the idea totally. And Armaan kept at it, bless him.

The floodgates now seemed open, cliched though that sounded. She began to think how utterly miserable her parents must have been when she first moved into being rebellious, then noncooperative and finally just plain ridiculous in leaving them without even a glance back.

How they went through the seemingly impossible task of keeping their calm when she raged so unfairly, and continuing to encourage her to learn and educate herself, while continuing to teach her by example, all the things they had always done.

She did not stop to think if she was overreacting even when her overwrought Mother would break down and cry, saying that she was a bad mother who couldn't teach her properly. She was the person who was so talented and capable and yet had chosen to stay home and bring up her children. She always said she wanted to teach them all she knew and made every effort to make them well rounded individuals. Respect, capability, affection, talent, caring, brilliant tenaciousness, all had to be balanced and honed to a fine precision, she used to say.

So much travel was planned so they could see the widest variety of places and the widest possible range of experiences to store away.

How her Mother must have felt when she told her to make a better choice and not bother her so much- who would want to be her mum's clone? Not Aurora. That was among all that she threw at her Mother.

Could she, Aurora, not have seen the innumerable number of ways her parents took care of her, and sometimes even when they could ill afford it. Her mother sold her jewellery one time to pay school fees. She didn't hesitate one moment before doing it.

And she had been carrying this torch of misguided thought for so long. Blaming them particularly her Mother, for everything and more that she thought or felt she had to go through.

Did she not think she should have stopped to think, they were first time parents too. They were very intelligent people and extremely well qualified too. And everyone felt they were so sensible and took their advice, including her own friends. That should have told her something surely?

She called them idiots and asked them to stop interfering in her life. How pathetic was that?

She was blaming her lack of proper upbringing, or so she felt, for her hesitation to marry Armaan and even think of a family life with him, all of this and more on her parents.

Boy, this rotten way of thinking seemed to go so deep.

As the train rushed through the night, her thoughts started to now arrange themselves in the proper order with the correct balance that was so lacking in her assessment all this time. Somehow she began to feel lighter and she could feel the bits of barricade she has erected around herself, and held it in place all these years with the nails of ill feeling, fall along the sides of the track. She felt herself move forward towards the destination. Her family at her parental home. The warmth of reality began to weave a cloak of memories again around her, this time, she saw things in the right perspective. This, finally, made sense.

Parents may perhaps not explain their actions or think children are grown enough, well, it would seem that way at least. About her parents anyway. But that wasn't any indication of their affection or complete commitment to parenting.

Holding this new cloak close, she slept.

Fresh and early she woke, Aurora, while the dawn tugged gently at the strings to dislodge the layer of pre-morning darkness, ready to spread her soft glow in a million myriad shades of pink, blue, purple and orange.

Dressed in a tic as was her custom, she went along to the restaurant carriage and settled in for breakfast. She was musing over what she needed to do straightaway. She needed to, first of all, call Armaan and tell him she had crossed the bridge and was home. She needed to tell him she was ready to settle into a more permanent relationship with him.

The attendant brought her a tea to begin and as she stirred the sugar in, took it with milk and sugar, she did; a gent lowered himself into the place set opposite, with the usual "good morning".

"Good Morning", she replied.

As if encouraged, he asked the next question. "Travelling for work", he asked, seeing she was alone. "No", she said, with a smile that widened as she spoke, "I'm going home".

About the Author

Lata Gullapalli is an investment banker by profession, specialising in mergers and acquisitions. She has worked in investment banking for over 20 years in South Asia, Russia and the U.K.

She advises companies on mergers and acquisitions, financial restructure and capital raising. She has designed products for raising capital. She has set up and run start-up companies, devising strategy and funding for them. She has led teams into joint ventures and taken a company public with an initial public offering.

She is an author, with published works and is currently writing her first full novel. She likes to absorb the emotions that people bring with them into her writing in the different situations, and seek or show the way forward.

She also works with NGOs in the U.K. and in India that are focused primarily on and are involved in, child protection, education for the girl child and orphaned children.

She lives in London.

Printed and bound by CPI Group (UK) Ltd, Croydon, CR0 4YY